THE KISS

He put his finger under my chin and lifted my face up to look at him. Our faces were shadowed in the dim light filtering out from the windows, and I was glad, for I knew my eyes would betray the panic growing inside me.

When he stepped closer to me, I had the insane desire to pull away from him, race up the stairs, and make a wish in Millicent's mirror. I'd wish I knew how to kiss. I needed magic. Maybe more than magic . . .

Other Avon Flare Books by
Ann Gabhart

ONLY IN SUNSHINE

Wish Come True

Ann Gabhart

AN AVON  FLARE BOOK

WISH COME TRUE is an original publication of Avon Books. This work has never before appeared in book form.

AVON BOOKS
A division of
The Hearst Corporation
105 Madison Avenue
New York, New York 10016

First Avon Flare Printing: November 1988

AVON FLARE TRADEMARK REG. U.S. PAT. OFF. AND IN OTHER COUNTRIES, MARCA REGISTRADA, HECHO EN U.S.A.

Printed in the U.S.A.

K-R 10 9 8 7 6 5 4 3 2 1

To my mother with love and appreciation

Chapter 1

"Make a wish, Lyssie," Robbie yelled as Mom sat the birthday cake with its fifteen flaming candles down in front of me. "Then I'll help you blow out the candles."

"I wish you'd let me blow out my own candles," I said.

Robbie's face fell, and he stopped jumping up and down for almost ten seconds before he got caught up in the excitement of the birthday cake again. "You're not supposed to tell your wish out loud. Are you, Daddy?"

"I don't think that was Lyssie's birthday wish, Robbie." Dad grinned at me. "She surely can come up with one better than that."

"But she can't say it out loud. She can't tell anybody, and she has to blow out all the candles or it won't come true." Robbie ran around behind me to get a better look at the cake.

From her chair at the end of the table, Aunt Reva said, "If she doesn't hurry up, there'll be so much candle wax on the cake, it won't be fit to eat."

"Now, Aunt Reva," Dad said gently. "A little candle wax never hurt anybody, and a birthday wish is a special thing that takes some thought."

"Humph," Aunt Reva said. "If wishes were horses . . ."

"Beggars would ride," Dad finished for her. "Even so, Aunt Reva, birthday wishes are fun."

I stared at the candles until their flames became a blur while I shut out the voices around me. Then, wishing as hard as I could, I blew. The flames flickered and began going out. After I used my last bit of breath to puff out the final candle on the edge of the cake, I sank back in my chair.

"Now your wish will come true," Robbie pronounced, a satisfied smile on his face. At six, he still believed in Santa Claus, the tooth fairy, and birthday wishes.

This was my fifteenth birthday wish. Each year the candles were a little harder to blow out, and it was a little harder to believe the wish I made would come true.

Mom helped me pick the candles off the chocolate cake she'd decorated with white icing and a blue-ribboned number fifteen surrounded by red music notes. She'd said that next year I could have a party and invite all my friends, but not this year, what with Aunt Reva being sick and just getting used to us being here.

I don't know why Mom worried about it since I didn't know anyone in Brookdale to invite to a party anyway. So just in case birthday wishes worked, that's what I'd wished for. A few friends, please. A boyfriend would be nice, too, I thought now as I began slicing the cake.

That didn't sound so hard, but everything this year was difficult. Everything had changed since I'd blown out the fourteen candles on my last birthday cake. We'd moved into this house to take care of my great-aunt Reva who didn't have any family—except my father—and had even less money. All she had was this big, old house. I let my eyes touch her face briefly as I handed her a piece of cake.

She was scowling as usual. Although she'd been the one to ask us to move in with her, she didn't act like she wanted us there any more than I wanted to be there. But Dad said the arrangement would be good for all of us, that it was good to help out your elders when they were sick, and that having us around might make Aunt Reva feel better.

I was beginning to doubt that since I had yet to see her smile even once. I stayed away from her whenever I could, but sometimes I had to sit with her while Mom went to the grocery.

Now as Aunt Reva looked at her piece of cake, she said, "What a lot of trouble you went to, Vivien." She frowned. "It must have taken you hours to decorate that cake, and now we're just going to destroy your artistry in a few minutes. Then all that time will have been wasted."

"We've had the pleasure of seeing it first," Mom said evenly.

"Time's never wasted making something beautiful," Dad said cheerfully. "And it is beautiful, just like our birthday girl."

"Pretty doesn't last long," Aunt Reva said, glancing over at me.

"Long enough to enjoy." Dad smiled and winked at me. "Now eat up, Aunt Reva, and then it'll be time for Alyssa's presents. We'll get to see if any of them are the answer to her wish."

I imagined him bringing in a package of people who I could wind up and take to school with me to be my friends, and I had to laugh.

"Not the kind of wish that comes in a box, eh?" Dad said as he handed me two brightly wrapped gifts.

I carefully peeled off the tape to keep from ripping

3

the gift wrap while Robbie scooted closer, hardly able to keep from grabbing the package and tearing into it himself. But when I folded back the tissue paper to reveal a sweater, he went back to his cake and ice cream, muttering, "Clothes."

The second box held a bracelet that Dad had, no doubt, found in a pawn shop. When I held it up, the various colored stones strung together on a delicate chain caught the light. The bracelet looked fragile and old but beautiful, too, and it was just the sort of thing that would catch Dad's eye. As I fastened it around my wrist, I wondered where I'd ever wear it. It wasn't exactly the kind of bracelet I could wear to school.

Robbie jumped up again and ran up the stairs. In a few seconds he was back with the picture he'd drawn especially for me. "See, I even wrote out happy birthday," he pointed out proudly.

I pretended to know what the picture was. "Thank you, Robbie. It's very pretty, and thank you, Mom and Dad, for the other things. The cake and everything."

"Aren't you going to ask what I got you, Alyssa?" Aunt Reva said.

"I didn't think you'd feel up to shopping," I said.

"Of course I didn't shop, but not all presents come from stores," she said. "There are a great many nice things stored in the attic. You can pick something out for your room if you like. I seem to remember a nice lamp up there."

I tried to sound enthusiastic, but it didn't ring true. Mom jumped in. "That's a wonderful idea, Aunt Reva, and very kind of you. I'm sure Alyssa will be able to find something she likes, and it'll mean a lot to her because it was once yours."

I smiled brightly. I couldn't wait to go drag down some piece of junk from the attic to put in my room.

"One more present," Mom said. She went into the kitchen and came back with a basket of oranges. The heart-shaped basket, woven of white oak strips, was different from any I'd seen Mom make before.

"It's beautiful, Mom," I said as I took it from her. Since she made baskets to sell at gift shops and Dad sold fresh produce at his fruit stand, getting a basket of fruit had become a tradition on my birthday.

"I picked the very best oranges out of the boxes I got in yesterday. My customers will have to do with second best this week," Dad said.

"But they're all orange," I said.

Dad smiled. "Not a red one among them."

"Whatever are you two talking about?" Mom asked.

"Nothing. Just a private joke between Lyssie and me," Dad said quickly.

I gathered up my presents and went around and kissed everybody, even Aunt Reva. She still didn't smile, and Robbie rubbed away his kiss.

Then I escaped up the stairs to my room. I set the basket of oranges on my chest, glad that Dad hadn't explained about our little joke. It had to do with wishing, too. When I first began helping Dad in his fruit stand, I'd wished oranges could be red and apples orange and bananas purple. Dad used to let me search through each new box of fruit to see if I could find a red orange.

Of course I never did. Oranges were often green but never red. If they'd been red, they would have been called reds, Dad would say with a grin and then ask if I could imagine drinking red juice for breakfast. Then he'd wonder whether, if oranges were reds,

5

we'd call the color red orange, or if oranges were red that then I'd want reds to be orange.

Smiling, I picked up an orange out of the basket. I didn't wish oranges were red anymore. I wished for more important things, like friends and making the chorus at Brookdale High and having money to buy the kinds of clothes all the other kids wore.

Now I wished I didn't have to go up to the attic and pick out something to bring down to my room. But I'd have to. Dad had said that since Aunt Reva was sick, we should go out of our way to keep from hurting her feelings.

I climbed the steep, narrow stairs to the attic. The late afternoon sunshine coming through a small window in the end of the attic cast a dim light across the room, and I hoped I'd be able to find the lamp Aunt Reva had mentioned before it got too dark to see.

I hadn't been up to the attic since we'd moved in because Dad had said we shouldn't nose around in Aunt Reva's things. Besides I'd imagined the attic to be dusty and full of cobwebs. The cobwebs and dust were there in plenty along with just about everything else you could think of.

Tattered magazines and books were piled high on broken-down chairs and tables while boxes were stacked all over the floor. I lifted the top of one box, disturbing generations of dust, to find it full of old newspapers. The date of the top paper was July 5, 1919, and the front page was covered with stories about Brookdale's Independence Day parade.

I laid the paper back in the box and rubbed its dry, dusty feel off my fingers. Why would anyone save so many old newspapers?

But then, from the looks of the attic, Aunt Reva had saved everything. I spotted a lamp in the corner. With a new shade it might not be too bad, I thought as I held it up for a better look. As long as it pleased Aunt Reva.

She wasn't very easy to please. Mom said it was because she was old and set in her ways, but Dad said Aunt Reva had always been a little peculiar and not very friendly. After Uncle Hewitt died, she had broken off all contact with his side of the family, including his namesake, Dad.

So I hadn't even known there was an Aunt Reva in the family until Mom told me we were going to move in with her.

"The house needs a little fixing up, but it's big and airy and we won't have to pay rent," Mom had said. "We checked and though the schools are small, they have a fine reputation. You'll be able to make lots of new friends, Alyssa."

"But what will Dad do about his fruit stand?" I'd asked. Dad had run a stand in the middle of the city for years.

"He'll just have to find a location close to Aunt Reva's house. You can sell fruit anywhere the same as you can make baskets anywhere," Mom had said as she shaped the ribs of a new basket. "A new place will be a challenge, a good change perhaps." Mom had looked up from her basket out the window at her bird feeder. "Brookdale's sort of a country town. Maybe I'll spot some new birds."

A birder, Mom kept a lifetime list of birds she'd seen. Once she'd driven a hundred miles to spot a rare bird sighted in the area by another birder, but since then she hadn't been able to add a new bird to her list.

I looked toward the window. Here she ought to have plenty of chances to see some different birds. There might even be bats here in the attic. Aunt Reva acted batty enough herself sometimes.

As I stood up to go downstairs to show Aunt Reva the lamp and thank her again, a slanting ray of sunlight caught in an oval mirror over in the corner. I moved my head back and forth to try to see the flash of light again, but no sunlight hit the mirror now.

When I went closer for a better look, I saw the ancient trunk and forgot about the mirror. Its straps were rotted with age, and the top groaned as I lifted it. The trunk was full of old clothes, and their musty smell made me sneeze as I pulled out the dresses for a closer look. One dress, black velvet with bead buttons and a white crocheted collar, was wrapped in tissue paper and was much smaller than the others. Shaking it out, I held the dress up to me. Although it wasn't a child's dress, it was tiny. Could the Aunt Reva I knew downstairs have once been so small?

I caught sight of myself in the mirror and wished I could see her in the black dress before I folded it back into the tissue paper.

On the bottom of the trunk in a box with torn and flattened corners I found a long coil of reddish brown hair and a picture of two young girls. Neither of them wore smiles, but one had on the black velvet dress.

She was pretty. Her long hair was caught back away from her face, and even though the picture had no color, I knew that was her hair in the box.

It couldn't be Aunt Reva. This girl looked much too delicate. The girl beside her was bigger, more practical looking. She, too, wore what must have been a black dress, but it had no touch of lace or decoration. I stared hard at her and decided she might be Aunt Reva.

After placing the picture and the coil of hair back in the box, I put everything back into the trunk exactly the way I'd taken it out. Aunt Reva wasn't able to climb up the stairs to the attic, but I still felt like

I'd been poking around in things she might want me to stay out of. Robbie and I had already been warned to keep out of her bedroom and the room she called the parlor. Both were full of her keepsakes.

The things in this trunk were keepsakes, too. In her mind they might be as untouchable as the things in her room.

To shut the lid of the trunk I had to move the mirror, really looking at it for the first time since the trunk had grabbed all my attention with the mystery of what it contained. Nothing was hidden in the mirror, but now that I looked at it, I saw how pretty it was.

Aunt Reva had said I could pick out anything I wanted in the attic, and this mirror with its gilded, ornate frame was much nicer than the lamp. When I rubbed the dust off the mirror with my shirttail, the glass gleamed.

I had to have it.

Downstairs, Aunt Reva stared at the mirror when I asked her if I could have it instead of the lamp. "Millicent's mirror," she said. "It might not be a good choice."

"Why?"

She pulled her eyes away from her reflection in the mirror. "What?" she said.

"I asked why the mirror wouldn't be a good choice. It's still pretty."

"Yes, pretty. Too pretty." She stared at me a minute before letting her eyes drop to her hands in her lap. "Like you," she added softly.

Talking to her was beginning to make me feel creepy, so I said, "If you don't want me to have the mirror, I'll take it back to the attic and get the lamp."

She looked up as if surprised to see me still standing there in front of her. Her eyes touched the mirror, but she quickly averted them. "What?"

"I said I'll take it back up to the attic if you want me to."

"No, no. I said you could have whatever you wanted. I'd forgotten about Millicent's mirror, but surely after all these years . . . And it couldn't have been the mirror anyway. It couldn't have been."

I couldn't make sense of anything she was saying except that the mirror had once belonged to Millicent. As much as I wanted to get away from Aunt Reva, I couldn't keep from asking, "Who's Millicent?"

"Millicent? Yes, Millicent." Aunt Reva's chin dropped down on her chest. After another minute she said, "Go tell Vivien I'm tired. I want to go to bed."

"Okay," I said. It didn't really matter who Millicent was anyway. I had the mirror. That was the important thing. Before I turned to go, I made myself say, "Thank you, Aunt Reva. It's one of the nicest birthday presents I ever got."

"Nice," she repeated after me, but there was nothing nice or pleasant about her voice.

As I went out of the room, I could hear her muttering to herself, but I only caught a few words and nothing that made any sense. Out in the hall, I took a deep breath to get the smell of age and sickness out of my nose, then caught sight of my reflection in the mirror and felt better immediately.

Chapter 2

The mirror fit on the wall like it belonged there, and I wondered if this had once been Millicent's room, whoever she was. While he'd hung the mirror for me, I'd asked Dad if he knew anything about a Millicent, but he hadn't.

It didn't really matter. The mirror was mine now, and it brightened up my room better than a lamp could have. I didn't know why. It wasn't very large, but after I cleaned it up, the glass seemed extra bright and had a way of catching light and bouncing sparkles off the walls and ceiling.

But mostly I liked it because I didn't have to wait my turn for the bathroom mirror anymore to get ready for school. I could take my time and wish and dream about the day ahead.

My birthday wish had yet to come true. I went to school every day and smiled and tried to look like the kind of person anybody would love to talk to, but nobody had exactly rushed over to be my best friend.

I'd made the chorus, but at Brookdale High that wasn't much of an achievement. All I'd had to do to be in chorus was put chorus on my schedule. That practice made for a variety of voices and ability and a chorus that didn't come up to the standard of the one at my old high school in the city.

Mr. Anderson, my former chorus director, had

winced at the hint of a sour note, and two sour notes was reason enough to stop and begin again. But Mr.—believe it or not—Birdsong was practically the opposite. If we sang a line well, he'd get this beatific look on his face as though we'd just accomplished a major miracle.

I told Mom I didn't think singing in Mr. Birdsong's choir was going to help develop my voice and that I really wanted private lessons.

"I know, dear." She was putting the finishing touches on one of her baskets. "As soon as your father gets started in his new location, maybe we'll be able to afford lessons for you." She looked up. "And it's not like you can't practice singing on your own. You don't really have to have a teacher."

It had been like that ever since I could remember. Just wait a while till there was more money, no matter what it was that I asked for. There was never more money.

Dad said we had plenty, and I knew he was right. I didn't really care whether or not we were rich. Still a little extra money would be nice, at least enough so I could have voice lessons and maybe get a salon haircut instead of just letting Mom trim the ends of my hair. But I had no reason to expect things to change just because I was older.

Now I stared at myself in Millicent's mirror as I combed my hair in the style I'd worn for years and wished that things weren't always the same, that something would happen, that I could be prettier. Girls who were pretty always had lots of friends. Take Marci Reid. She was pretty and blonde and had friends trailing her for miles down the hall as she walked between classes.

Impulsively I pushed my bangs back off my forehead. It was time for a change. A coating of hair spray kept the bangs back, and I did look different. I wouldn't go so far as to say pretty, but with my hair swept back away from my face, my eyes seemed larger and almost a smoky blue instead of their regular gray color. My eyes were my best feature, if I had a best feature. On the whole I was pretty average looking. Not bad, just nothing special.

Putting down my comb, I stared at my face a minute longer. I wish I were pretty, I whispered to the mirror. Really pretty, so that people would notice me like they noticed Marci Reid.

"What are you doing?" Robbie asked from the doorway.

"Fixing my hair." I turned away from the mirror.

"It doesn't take me that long to comb my hair."

"That's because you don't care what you look like."

"Don't I look okay?" A funny little frown wrinkled Robbie's forehead.

"You look okay for a Robin." I put my hand on his head. "Did Dad send you up here to get me?"

"Yeah. Mama's sick."

"Sick?"

"She threw up." Robbie's eyes got wider.

"Oh no. I hope she doesn't have a virus."

"What's a virus?" Robbie asked as he went down the stairs in front of me.

"Something you can catch, and I can't be sick today. We're going to do solos in chorus."

As we were going out the back door, Mom came into the kitchen and waved goodbye to us. She was pale but smiling. A private, quiet little smile. I didn't remember ever feeling like smiling when I had a stomach virus.

Dad made up silly songs as he drove us to school. Robbie was laughing so hard by the time we reached his school that he could hardly get out of the truck. I could remember spilling out of the truck the same way and then sitting through the endless hours of school hardly able to wait until I could go to the fruit stand and listen to Dad and his customers talking. Many of them were regulars, and they would lean on the counter for hours and discuss what Dad called why-is-it-so questions.

They came to my father for the talk as much as for the produce. I wondered what they were doing now that Dad was gone.

"You're not smiling much this morning, Lyssie," Dad said as he pulled out into the traffic and headed toward the high school.

"Mom was sick when we left," I said.

"I know." He kept smiling, a strange, silly little smile.

"You look like you're happy about that."

His face grew sober. "No, not at all." But then the smile sneaked back.

"Mom won't be able to take care of Aunt Reva if she's sick." I thought of the chorus solos and how hard I'd worked on the song we were to sing, but I made myself say, "Maybe I should go back and help her today."

Dad reached over and patted my hand. "I would never have believed Lyssie the wisher would become Lyssie the serious."

"Somebody has to be."

Dad laughed. "And what do you mean by that, Alyssa?" He said every syllable of my name distinctly.

"I don't know." I flushed a little.

"Yes, you do, and didn't I always tell you to say what you think no matter how wild and unreasonable or sane that might be?" When I didn't say anything, he went on. "You mean that your mother gets so caught up in her birdwatching and I in my poems that neither of us has time for the serious things in life. But how do you know, Lyssie, that birds and poems aren't the real serious things in life?"

"I guess I don't, but that doesn't help Mom if she doesn't feel like waiting on Aunt Reva today."

Dad turned into the school. "Don't worry about your mother, Lyssie. I'll go home and help her with Aunt Reva until she's feeling better."

"Who's going to run the fruit stand?"

"Nobody buys fruit in the morning anyway, and you can come help me this afternoon. A pretty face like yours behind the counter is sure to boost sales."

"Oh, Daddy. I'm not pretty."

He pulled to a stop in front of the school. "No, I guess not," he said. "Pretty is for kittens and babies. Maybe I should have said beautiful."

I couldn't keep from smiling back at him as I got out of the truck. "Oh, go home and write a poem."

"Maybe I will if Aunt Reva sleeps a while. Maybe on the special beauty of this particular moment in time."

He was already thinking about the poem as he pulled away, and I hoped he'd make it home without hitting something. Dad sometimes got a poem published, but he rarely ever got paid for one. He said he didn't write his poems for money, only for the love of the way words could awaken feelings.

I sighed as I went in the door to join the crowd of kids rushing to their homerooms. Why couldn't I have an ordinary family like everybody else instead of a father who sold fruit and a mother who wove baskets?

I watched the kids passing me in the hall. Brookdale was a small school, and I already knew the faces of most of the kids. I even knew some of their names, but I didn't know what their parents did for a living. I'd never even thought about it before now.

As I pushed my way through to my locker, I began to match the kids up with some kind of occupation. This one had a doctor for a father, and that girl's mother worked at a grocery store. I assigned occupations as fast as I could think them up until I spotted Marci Reid.

She looked beautiful, as always. Her father did something important. Maybe he was a lawyer or psychiatrist or surgeon. He obviously made plenty of money. Marci had worn a different outfit to school every day so far. Me, I had maybe five decent shirts to wear with my jeans and a lot of homemade skirts and dresses.

Mom said clothes didn't matter, that it was what was on the inside of a person that counted instead of what was on the outside. That sounded good at home in the kitchen, but not so good in the halls at school.

It mattered. And it mattered if you were pretty. That mattered even more than what your mother and father did for a living.

When I opened my locker, I caught sight of my face in the little mirror I'd stuck to the inside of the door. For some reason it was like looking at someone I didn't know, and I decided I really didn't look that bad. Maybe not exactly pretty, but what was it Dad had said? Beautiful. Grinning at the thought, I slammed the locker shut. As I rushed toward homeroom, the song I was to sing in chorus began to run through my head.

Chorus was the last class of the day. All the girls sang the same song, so by the time ten girls had taken their turn, we were all sick of it. Mr. Birdsong sat in the back of the room and kept his eyes closed as each girl sang. Then he would nod solemnly, scribble furiously on a piece of paper, and call out the next name.

Marci Reid sang before me. She had a nice voice, not really strong, but she hit every note perfectly. Not only did Mr. Birdsong keep his eyes open while she sang, everybody in the chorus seemed to sit up and listen. She was obviously the star of the ensemble, and I thought it wasn't fair that she could be so pretty and popular and sing well besides.

I reminded myself I wasn't in competition with her. Mr. Anderson at my old school had always stressed that voices in a choir didn't compete, they blended.

Still I was nervous as I took her place in front of the class. But then the music began, and I let myself be carried away into the song.

As I returned to my seat, I glanced out of the corner of my eye toward Mr. Birdsong. Instead of scribbling on his paper, he was staring straight at me with such a surprised look on his face that I stopped in the middle of the aisle and asked, "Did I do something wrong?"

"No, no." He looked down at his paper. "No, no, Alicia. It is Alicia, isn't it?"

"Alyssa, sir."

"That was fine, Lissa. Very fine," he said as he bent over his paper again. But he still didn't write anything.

The next girl stood up to take my place at the front of the room, but even while she sang I kept feeling the other kids looking at me. I couldn't have been that bad, I told myself. Mr. Anderson had said I had a good voice, untrained but lovely anyway. He'd said with lessons there was no telling how good I might get. Of course he'd been the one giving the lessons, so maybe he just told me that in an attempt to get another student.

I was glad when Mr. Birdsong went back to closing his eyes as the girls sang through the song. He was a funny little man, sort of like a bird in the way he moved around so quickly and jerkily. The girl who sat beside me had told me that he'd been teaching music here at Brookdale for more years than anyone could remember.

When the bell rang, he hopped up and reminded the boys that they'd have to sing their solos the next day. I thought that was sure to be more fun than listening to the girls had been today. At least it would give me an excuse to stare at the guys, and I especially looked forward to staring at one of the boys.

Doug Clifton had to be the cutest boy at Brookdale High with his dark brown hair and blue eyes, and there was something special about his smile.

Of course when I'd seen him, he'd usually been smiling at Marci Reid. They were always together in the hall, obviously special friends.

I'd never been special friends with any boy.

I glanced around now before I went out of the chorus room to see if I could spot him. He was talking to Marci, and they were both looking over toward me.

When I jerked my eyes away from them, I met Mr. Birdsong's eyes. He smiled and bobbed his head at me. Embarrassed, I smiled back and then proceeded to bump into three chairs before I could get out of the room.

The hall was crowded with kids headed to their lockers, and I slipped in among them with a sigh of relief. Nobody was staring at me out here. Most of the kids didn't even know my name. I was just the new girl.

As if to prove me wrong, someone called out behind me, "Alyssa. Wait a minute."

Marci Reid, of all people, was running to catch up with me.

A little out of breath, she said, "I'm glad I caught you."

"Why's that?" I was too surprised to be polite.

"I wanted to talk to you, that's why." Marci laughed, and the beautiful blue of her eyes deepened.

I smiled back at her, not sure what I should say next.

Marci didn't seem to care whether I said anything or not as she raced on. "I just had to tell you what a fantastic job you did on the song. When you sang it, it sounded like a new song instead of the one we'd already heard a dozen times."

"You really think so?" I stopped at my locker. "The way everybody was staring at me, I thought I'd messed up big time."

"You didn't miss a note, but it was more than that. There's something about you when you sing." Her eyes narrowed as she looked at me. "Something different."

"Well, thanks, I guess," I said awkwardly as I began working the combination on my locker. "You sang well, too."

Marci brushed aside my compliment. "I've got a long way to go before I'm a great singer or anything, but my voice teacher says with work I might get better. Who's your voice teacher?"

"I don't take lessons."

"Really? Are you kidding?"

"No." I shoved my books in the locker. Then as I began to shut the locker door, I caught a glimpse of myself in the little mirror. I still looked different. My eyes were sparkling like Marci's, and though mine were definitely gray and not blue, that was all right. It was a nice gray. I slammed the door shut and turned to Marci.

"Well, gee, I'd better run," she said with a glance up at the clock in the hall. "Doug will be waiting for me, but I just wanted to tell you how good you did on the song. Maybe we can get together and practice sometime. I could even introduce you to Mr. Wilson, my voice teacher."

"I thought maybe you took lessons from Mr. Birdsong."

"Birdie? He's a sweet old thing, but he doesn't know what he's doing half the time." Laughing, she started off up the hall before she called over her shoulder, "See you tomorrow."

She rushed off to join Doug, the guy with the great smile. A smile a lot like hers. But I wasn't jealous. Instead I found myself wishing Marci and I could be friends.

As I went out into the hot afternoon sunshine, a song about wishing popped into my head, and I began humming as I walked downtown to Dad's fruit stand.

Chapter 3

That night I sat in front of Millicent's mirror and sang the song I'd sung in choir that day. When I finished that song, I sang another and then another.

The longer I watched myself in the mirror the more I felt like I was watching someone I didn't know and not myself at all, and after a while it was almost as if the person in the mirror were more alive than I was.

Every time I stopped singing, I could hear Dad talking downstairs and Robbie and Mom laughing. Everybody had been in high spirits at supper. Everybody, of course, except Aunt Reva.

I'd had the memory of singing my solo and talking to Marci Reid. Robbie had found a little girl named Joey to pal around with just down the street, and Mom had sighted a new bird.

She wasn't sick tonight. In fact she acted like she felt extra good, and she'd reassured me while we were clearing away the dishes that she hadn't had a virus. Then she had looked at Dad, and he'd gotten up and come around the table to kiss her. Laughing, Mom had pushed him lightly away.

"You're acting like teenagers," Aunt Reva spoke up crossly from her end of the table.

"But we are teenagers at heart sometimes," Dad said. "Don't you sometimes wish you could be a teenager again, Aunt Reva?" Dad smiled over at me.

"Young like Lyssie here, full of wishes and dreams and with everything ahead of you."

"Too much wishing is a bad thing." Aunt Reva's old eyes wandered around the walls and came to rest on me. "Did you put it up in your room, girl?" she asked suddenly.

"What?" I asked, though I knew at once what she was talking about.

"The mirror. Millicent's mirror," she said impatiently.

"Yes," I said.

"It's a lovely old mirror," Mom said. "I'm sure it must be antique, so if you've changed your mind about Alyssa having it, we'll understand."

"No, I don't want the thing. It should have been done away with when Millicent died."

"Who was Millicent?" I asked.

"My sister," Aunt Reva said.

"Did she die a long time ago?"

"Yes." Aunt Reva's eyes narrowed on me as she went on. "But you might as well stop with your questions. People and their endless questions. They think just because you're old that you like to talk."

"Most people do like to talk," Dad said mildly.

"That was always your problem, wasn't it, Hewitt?" she said, turning on him. "Too much talking, not enough doing. Pretty words won't pay bills."

While I helped Mom with the dishes she told me that I shouldn't let anything Aunt Reva said bother me.

"I don't," I said as I put the plates up in the cabinet.

"Good. She's not really a bad old lady underneath. It's just that she's lived alone for so long that she's having a hard time adjusting to us being here. Especially you children. Your noise gets on her nerves."

22

"I try to be quiet and not bother her."

"I know." Mom smiled a bit sadly. "And I suppose the reason she's cross is not really that simple. Maybe she sees you and remembers being young herself, and so hates being old and helpless now that she takes it out on everybody around her. She's just not very happy right now."

"And she doesn't want anybody else around her to be happy either, does she?"

"She does try to nip happiness in the bud," Mom agreed with a little laugh. "But I think she's met her match in your father. I wouldn't be a bit surprised if he doesn't get a laugh out of her before the month is gone."

"I don't think she knows how to laugh. I haven't even seen her smile yet."

"Then your father will teach her." Mom got a thoughtful look on her face. "He taught me to laugh again, you know. After my mother died, I didn't think anything would ever be good again. But it was. Hewitt and I got married, and then I had you and Robbie and now." She stopped and smiled.

"And now you've got Aunt Reva. That's not much to be happy about."

"Oh, there's always something to be happy about. Always something."

Now I could still hear Mom and Robbie laughing at Dad's stories downstairs, and I found myself smiling, too, even though I didn't know what story he was telling. I was still staring into the mirror, and I let the smile linger on my face. I believed I really was prettier today than I had been yesterday. I didn't know how that was possible, but it was true. At least when I looked into Millicent's mirror it was.

And hadn't Marci Reid run me down in the hall to

talk to me? I'd been at Brookdale High for weeks without her noticing me, and then right after I'd wished I was prettier, she'd not only noticed me, she'd made a special effort to talk to me.

I stared at my face in the mirror. You couldn't wish yourself prettier. Wishes like that just didn't come true. I wasn't sure anymore that any wishes came true. That was kid stuff, wishing on stars and crossing your fingers and pulling wishbones apart.

Yet I looked different. My eyes were grayer, my face slimmer. Surely just brushing my hair a different way couldn't make that much difference.

I laughed a little at myself and turned away from the mirror to start on my homework. Still, every time I glanced up from my history book, the mirror would catch my eye.

The next morning as I got ready for school, I kept thinking about Marci Reid. It would be so nice to have a girl like Marci for a friend.

I sat my brush down and looked at myself in the mirror. It had worked the day before. I'd wished I was prettier, and then I'd felt prettier all day. Maybe I should wish Marci was my friend.

Feeling more than a little silly, I whispered the words, "I wish Marci Reid and I were friends." Then I told myself it wasn't any sillier to make a wish in a mirror than it was to make wishes on stars or birthday candles. All wishes were silly. Or maybe the wishes weren't silly, just the wisher.

I grinned at myself self-consciously as I made one last brush at my bangs. It didn't take nearly as much hair spray to keep them back off my forehead this morning.

Downstairs, Robbie and Dad were already in the truck waiting for me. As I passed Mom at the table warming her hands around a cup of tea, I dropped a quick kiss on her cheek.

At the door, I hesitated before going out. "Are you okay, Mom?"

"Sure. I'm just feeling a little under the weather this morning. I'll be fine in a little bit." She waved me off with a smile. "Have a good day at school."

I hardly heard anything Dad and Robbie said as we rode to school. Something kept nudging at my memory, something about the way Mom had looked.

After Robbie got out, Dad and I rode on to the high school in silence. I was still thinking about Mom, and Dad was either writing a poem in his head or mulling over some problem. I didn't try to find out which.

As I climbed out of the truck in front of the school, I promised Dad I'd come help him at the stand again that afternoon. I thought that would give me a chance to ask him what was wrong with Mom.

Then home problems were pushed to the back of my mind when I went through the front door and spotted Marci Reid coming in the side door with Doug Clifton. She grinned at him and waved as she split off to go to her locker, which was close to mine.

Before I could think about why I shouldn't, I fell in beside her. "Hi," I said.

"Oh hi, Alyssa." Marci's smile didn't look a bit forced. "Aren't you glad we don't have to sing again today?"

"I like to sing."

"Yeah, me too, but it still puts you pretty much on the spot to have to get up in front of everybody by yourself like that." Marci made a face. "You get to feeling like you've got your blouse on backward or your jeans are unzipped."

25

I looked over at her in surprise. "You surely don't worry about how you look. You always look great."

She pushed back her blonde hair and laughed. "Only because I do worry so much."

"I worry, too, but it doesn't seem to do much good."

"Oh, Alyssa, you look nice. Especially when you sing. Even Doug said so."

"Doug said that?"

"Yeah. He doesn't want to sing this afternoon. I think he'd quit chorus if he thought old Birdie would ever forgive him." Marci laughed. "Doug says it would be different if Birdie had any reason for the solos, but we just get up every year and sing our solos and then that's the end of it."

"Then why does he have you do it?"

"He just always has, and with Birdie, what has always been done will continue to be done until time is no more."

The first bell rang then, and we had to run for our homerooms before the second bell rang.

At lunch I'd already sat down when I saw Marci going through the line. Three or four people waved at her, but she came straight to my table. "Hi," she said as she sat down. She picked up her fork and looked at her food. "Ugh. S.O.S. Same old slop."

She took a bite of her sandwich before she went on. "I say every day I'm going to bring my lunch from home, but it's too much trouble to get up in the morning and fix it."

"I used to take my lunch sometimes at my old school."

"I'll bet your mother fixed it for you, but my mother's not the domestic type. She can't even make a peanut butter sandwich."

"Anybody can make a peanut butter sandwich."

"Not my mother." Marci laughed.

"Then who does the cooking? Your father?"

"Daddy will make coffee if he has to, but other than that, forget it. No, we just make do with whatever we can pour out of a box or stick in a toaster for breakfast, and then Celina comes in to fix lunch and dinner."

I concentrated on my sandwich and didn't say anything. I'd never known anyone who had a cook. A cleaning lady maybe, but never a cook. Poor Mom, she had to be cook, cleaning lady, and now nursemaid to Aunt Reva. I remembered how pale she'd looked that morning, but quickly pushed the thought away.

After a few minutes, Marci asked, "How come you moved to Brookdale, Alyssa?"

"To stay with my father's aunt Reva."

"Miss Reva? The old lady who lives in that big house on the corner of Walnut?" Marci looked up at me in surprise. "I was always scared to death of her when I was a kid."

"Really?"

"It sounds kind of silly now when you think about it, but when you're a little kid you sort of look for something to make you feel creepy."

"Aunt Reva makes me feel creepy sometimes now," I said and then added quickly, "but I guess she can't help being cross. She's sick."

"If that's the reason she's cross, she's been sick ever since I can remember," Marci said. "And she's your aunt. I didn't know she had any family."

"Just us."

Marci put down her sandwich. "I'm embarrassed when I think of the mean things we used to do to her. We'd dare each other to run up on her porch at night and knock on her door. She'd get so mad that sometimes she'd make the police come out, but they never did anything.'' She nibbled on a chip and then asked, ''Did you ever do anything like that to some poor old person?''

''No.'' I thought of all Dad's elderly customers back in the city, and I wondered if anybody was letting Old Jim have free bananas now.

Marci put down the chip, and her cheeks reddened. ''I shouldn't have told you about it. You think I'm horrible.''

''No, I don't.'' I smiled to reassure her I didn't while at the same time a funny little thrill went through me because she cared enough about what I thought to actually blush.

''I was such a mean kid, but I'd never do anything like that now,'' Marci said. ''Maybe I could come over sometime and try to make amends.''

''Aunt Reva wouldn't want you to. She really doesn't like people bothering her.''

''She surely wouldn't mind me apologizing, and I'd like to come visit you sometime.''

''I guess that would be okay,'' I said, but I was relieved when Marci began talking about the history test we'd had that morning. I just couldn't imagine her at my house talking to Aunt Reva.

That afternoon in chorus, Doug Clifton was the last boy Mr. Birdsong called on to sing.

''Saving the best for last,'' Marci whispered as Doug took his place at the front of the room. Marci had come in the class and plopped down beside me. While the other boys had sung she'd been drawing rainbows and suns and clouds absentmindedly, but when Doug got up, she put her pen down and listened raptly. So did I.

The bell rang just as he was singing the last line of

the song. Marci looked over at me with shining blue eyes. "He's really good, isn't he?"

"He has a beautiful voice," I said.

"Doug's wonderful every way you can count," Marci said before she ran over to him.

As I gathered up my things and left the room, I wished I had the nerve to go over and say something to Doug, too. Maybe instead of Marci's friendship, I should have wished for courage in Millicent's mirror that morning.

I smiled at the thought as I walked out of the school and headed downtown toward Dad's fruit stand. Then the smile disappeared. The fact was I had wished Marci was my friend, and now it seemed to be a wish coming true.

Sunlight glanced off the windshield of a passing car. The mirror couldn't have had anything to do with it. It was crazy to even think such a thing.

I laughed at myself. What difference did it make anyway? Whether the mirror had granted my wish or not, I was still glad Marci wanted to be friends.

Humming a little under my breath, I went into the fruit stand. The little bell over the door tinkled, and Dad looked up from waiting on a customer to smile at me before turning all his attention back to helping the woman decide which kind of apples she wanted to buy.

Dad was good with people. By the time the woman went out the door, making the little bell jingle again, I knew she'd be back as much for Dad's smile and talk as for the fruit.

"This is going to be a great location," Dad said when we were alone. "People have been coming in from the businesses around here on their lunch breaks. I'm thinking about carrying some soft drinks and fruit juices."

He stopped and got a funny look on his face before he went on. "I'm practically sounding ambitious. Don't tell your mother."

"Why not?" I asked.

He rearranged a few apples in the top tray. "I promised her years ago that I'd never get caught up in the rat race of making money."

"What's so bad about making money?"

"Nothing." Dad picked a bruised apple out of the tray. "Nothing at all, Lyssie, as long as you remember that thoughts and ideas are more valuable than money. If you don't think about anything except making money then sometimes you don't have time to think about important things. The poetry of real life. Do you understand?"

"You're the poet. Not me," I said.

Dad smiled. "We're all poets in our own way. All of us writing the poetry of our lives. And I don't want the poem of my life to be punctuated with dollar signs."

"I doubt if selling soft drinks will add that many dollar signs." I began taking some oranges out of a box and spreading them behind the ones already on the shelf. I hoped Dad would let it drop, but he didn't.

"You're a verse in my poem, Lyssie, and so is Robbie and now—"

The bell jangled over the door and four people came in at once, filling the little store up. Dad looked at me as if he wanted to say more, but he couldn't with so many people there. Still, even while he was waiting on the people, I'd catch his eyes on me, eyes that held a hint of worry.

Finally in the truck going home, Dad said, "I've got something to tell you, Alyssa." He kept his eyes on the road.

After a quick glance over at his face, I stared out

30

the window and watched the houses passing. We were driving through a nice neighborhood, and I thought Marci might live in one of the big houses. Her cook would be setting dinner on the table for Marci and her family. I wondered if Marci had any brothers or sisters.

Dad kept talking. "You know how I was saying you were a verse in the poem of my life." He reached over and patted my hand. "One of the best verses I've ever written. And Robbie, too. The two of you make your mother and me rich the way money never could. And now we're going to write a new verse."

I turned slowly to look at Dad, but I wasn't really seeing him. I was seeing Mom's pale face and their secretive smiles at one another.

"Your mother's going to have another baby." His words hung in the air between us.

Chapter 4

"She's too old," I finally said.

Dad smiled. "We're not that old, Lyssie, and we've been wanting another baby for a long time."

A baby, of all things. I should have guessed. Mom was sick before Robbie was born, too, very sick at the end. "But it might be dangerous for her like with Robbie," I said.

Dad squeezed my hand. "The doctors said what happened with Robbie wouldn't happen again, and we'll make sure your mother takes care of herself and gets enough rest."

"How can she with Aunt Reva to take care of? This just doesn't seem like a very good time to be having a baby."

"Maybe not, but babies pick their own time to come along, and we'll work something out." Dad glanced over at me. "You came along when we were maybe too young, and we were glad. We're just as glad about this one, and we want you to be glad, too."

I swallowed hard, but I couldn't think of a thing to say.

Dad was quiet for a second before he went on. "Your mother is a little worried that you might feel embarrassed to have a mother expecting a baby, but I told her you'd be as excited as we are. Of course we'll all have to help your mother out more around the house and with Aunt Reva.''

"I've always helped around the house." I tried to go on and say that I was happy about the baby, but I couldn't.

Dad didn't seem to notice as he smiled and squeezed my hand again. "I knew I could count on you, Lyssie. If only all my poems were as lovely as you."

To keep from thinking too much about Mom having a baby, I looked away from him back out the window. We were almost to Aunt Reva's house. "I miss the old place," I said suddenly. "The old customers."

"I know," Dad said softly. "I keep expecting Old Jim to come in for his banana every day." He shook himself a little. "But there are some nice people here in Brookdale, too."

"It's not the same."

Dad looked over at me. "Nothing ever is. And that's good." His face grew thoughtful. "Just imagine how life would be if nothing ever changed. No one could be born, and no one could die. Everybody would stay the same age they were whenever things stopped changing. You'd never learn anything new or forget anything old. The flowers that were blooming would keep blooming forever like plastic replicas of themselves."

"Stop. It sounds awful."

"So you believe you'll take the challenge of change," Dad said. "That's good. We really don't have much choice."

Up ahead I saw Aunt Reva's big brick house, half-hidden from the street by three huge maple trees. Everything about the house, from the weathered red bricks to the dark narrow windows, looked old.

"I'll bet this house hasn't changed much," I said as we pulled into the drive.

"Oh, but it has, Lyssie." Dad stopped the truck and smiled a little as he stared at the house. "I used to love coming here when I was a kid. Uncle Hewitt liked children, and he was always playing with us. See over there. He put up a tire swing for us in that tree." Dad pointed at the maple farthest away from the house. "Grass didn't grow under it for years."

"I'll bet Aunt Reva didn't like that much."

"She was younger then and she took all the noise and commotion in fairly good spirits."

"Are you saying she enjoyed having a bunch of kids running through her house?"

Dad's smile slipped away as he answered, "She wanted to, but something always held her back. Uncle Hewitt used to fuss at her sometimes, tell her to jump on in and enjoy living."

"And did she?"

"No. She'd get that look on her face that wasn't quite a smile and back away a little more. I felt it even as a child. But Uncle Hewitt never gave up."

"He sounds nice."

"He was." Dad shifted the truck back into gear and drove on into the garage. "The last time I saw him, he knew he was dying and he made me promise not to forget about Aunt Reva, to keep trying to get her to enjoy living."

"And did you?" I asked as I got out of the truck.

"For a while. I'd come visit and she'd sit with me in the parlor and wish I'd go away." Dad looked over at me. "You've even been here several times with your mother and me when you were barely walking. We had to watch you like a hawk to make sure you didn't break any of Aunt Reva's trinkets. But finally Aunt Reva came right out and asked us to quit coming, so

34

we did. That was almost fourteen years ago, and I suppose I wouldn't ever have come back if Aunt Reva hadn't had her stroke and discovered she needed family after all.''

''She could have gone to a home.''

''No one ever wants to go to a nursing home, and this house has always been Aunt Reva's home. She inherited it from her parents. Take her away from it, and she probably wouldn't last long.'' Dad shook himself a little. ''Besides I should have never quit coming to see her in the first place.''

''I guess you didn't have much choice.''

''Choices are like changes. Inevitable. But we don't always make the right ones. Nevertheless, fate has given me a chance to keep my promise to Uncle Hewitt after all.''

''You can't expect Aunt Reva to enjoy living now.'' I thought of Aunt Reva's face creased permanently into a scowl.

''Why not?'' Dad said as he put his arm around me and we headed for the kitchen door. Back here the windows were full of light and warmth and welcome.

''You know how she is. She doesn't want to be happy.''

''Oh, Aunt Reva's not really so bad. She kind of likes us being here.''

''That's what you say.''

''That's what I know. And when the baby comes along she'll see it and have to love it. How could anybody not love a baby?'' Dad squeezed my shoulders before we went into the kitchen where Mom and Robbie were getting out the dishes to set the table.

Mom looked up at Dad who nodded just the barest bit, and then she looked at me. I knew they had planned on Dad telling me about the baby today, and

35

I knew she was waiting for me to say something. The right words wouldn't come. Instead I said, "Are you feeling okay, Mom? I can finish up dinner if you want me to."

"It's all ready," she said brightly. "We just lack setting the table and helping Aunt Reva to her chair."

"I'll go get her," I volunteered, hardly able to believe my ears. But I had to get away from Mom's eyes.

I was glad when dinner was over and the dishes were washed so I could escape to my room. I needed time to get used to the idea of Mom having a baby before I could talk about it.

Dad came to the living room door as I started up the stairs. Behind him I could see Mom reading to Robbie on the couch and Aunt Reva in her chair staring down at her hands.

"The dishes all done?" he said. "That didn't take long."

"There weren't many." It felt odd to be so stiff talking to Dad. I'd always been able to talk to him about anything, and now I couldn't even talk about washing the dishes without feeling uncomfortable.

"How about a game of rummy?"

"I've got homework," I said.

"Well, I guess you'd better go get at it then." Dad's smile suddenly looked as stiff as mine felt. "We can play cards another time."

Mom kept reading to Robbie, but Aunt Reva's eyes fastened on me like claws. "It's Millicent's wretched mirror," she said.

Dad turned to her. "What are you talking about, Aunt Reva? Mirrors. I think it has more to do with being fifteen," he said as he looked back at me. "Lyssie's on a quest of discovery—the discovery of self."

I kept my eyes on Aunt Reva, who stared a hole through me in return. "What do you mean?" I asked her.

"You'll find out." Aunt Reva dropped her eyes back to her hands in her lap.

Dad laughed. "Why, Aunt Reva, I think you're trying to sound mysterious."

Her eyes were shut, and she wouldn't look up. I knew she'd sit that way until two minutes before the clock chimed nine. Then she'd demand to be put to bed.

"I really do have homework," I said.

"I know you do, Lyssie," Dad said.

I ran on up the stairs to my room, where I leaned against the door as if something had been chasing me. It might have been better to have played a game of rummy. Now Dad would think I didn't want to play cards with him, and Mom would think I wasn't happy about the baby, and who knew what Aunt Reva was thinking.

When I flipped on the light switch, the mirror caught the light and bounced it back at me. A welcome. The whole room was waiting for me.

I sat down at the little table in front of the mirror and ran my fingers over the gilded frame before I lightly touched the cool glass.

It was old, but still just a mirror like any other. It couldn't do anything special. Yet I'd wished to be pretty, and somehow I'd felt prettier. I'd wished Marci and I could be friends, and we'd talked like friends.

I stared at the mirror, a little afraid of my thoughts. I'd always been a wisher, but my wishes had rarely come true. So rarely that I'd often wished for a magic rock or pebble to hold or a ring to wear that would make my wishes come true. I touched the mirror again. Was it finally my magic token?

I jerked my fingers away with a little laugh. I was being silly.

Nothing wrong with me being a little silly. I could hear Dad's words echoing in my mind. "If everybody worried about being silly, then many of the great discoveries would have never been made. It's good to think silly sometimes."

I shook my head. Dad hadn't been talking about magic mirrors, but about theories like gravity and the world being round or the possibility that somewhere out there in the universe there was intelligent life.

I looked at the mirror. The theory of magic mirrors would be easy enough to test. All I had to do was make a wish and see if it came true.

I stared at the mirror for a long time while all kinds of crazy thoughts went through my head. At last, feeling more than silly, I whispered, "I wish my eyes were blue."

Then for one awful moment as I stared at my reflection in the mirror, I thought my eyes were changing, becoming someone else's eyes, turning blue. My heart clunked heavily back and forth inside my chest, and I squeezed my eyes shut for a moment before I opened them again. My own dark gray eyes stared back at me. Familiar, expected, mine.

I laughed at myself even as a tremble passed through me. The mirror caught the light and seemed to brighten almost as if it, too, were laughing.

With another look to be sure my eyes were still the right color, I turned away from the mirror. Millicent's mirror. But no matter what Aunt Reva said, it was a mirror and only a mirror. It couldn't change the color of my eyes. I sneaked one last peek at my familiar gray eyes before I started on my homework.

As I settled in the middle of the bed with my books spread out around me, I thought I had more to worry about than magic mirrors and what color my eyes were. I'd be better off spending my time worrying about Mom having a baby and me having a spooky old aunt who I'd have to take care of if Mom got sick. And Dad expected me to be happy about it all.

I couldn't understand how he could be happy about it. Babies were expensive besides being dangerous to get here. I stared at the wall while I remembered when Robbie was born.

At first I'd been as excited as Mom and Dad, but then Dad had had to take a job at night to make the extra money for the doctor. Sometimes days went by without me seeing him. On top of that, something had gone wrong, and Mom had spent the last few weeks of her pregnancy in the hospital. Dad had tried to reassure me, and while he was home I could believe everything was going to be all right. But once he'd gone off to work or to the hospital, I would wander around the house wishing Mom would come home while all my excitement about the baby disappeared.

Now it was all going to happen again, and even if they could be sure Mom wouldn't get sick like before, then there was still the problem of enough money for the baby. It was all very well not to want to devote your whole life to making money, but it wouldn't hurt to be a little more practical.

With a sigh, I opened my English book. There was nothing I could do about any of it anyway. Dad had never worried about being practical, and they both wanted the baby. I'd just be as practical as I could by doing whatever I could to help Mom, while at the same time I'd try not to let it spoil any of the good things that had begun to happen to me at school.

I didn't look in the mirror again until the next morning. Then with sunshine flooding through the window, my idea that it might be a magical mirror seemed like some kind of crazy dream.

If my eyes seemed to be a bit softer gray than usual, it was only the blue blouse I was wearing. A person's eye color couldn't change because of a wish. Wishes didn't work that way.

Still, wishing never hurt anything, and it was sort of fun even if it was far from practical. I grinned at myself in the mirror and wondered what I could wish for today. Just for fun. Suddenly I thought of Doug Clifton with his dark hair and blue eyes. I could think up a dozen wishes about him, but none of them could ever come true because he was Marci's boyfriend.

"I wish Doug Clifton wasn't Marci's boyfriend," I whispered to the mirror and then felt so foolish that I jumped up, grabbed my books, and ran down the stairs.

I was surprised to see Aunt Reva in the kitchen with Mom, who looked pale but said brightly, "Aunt Reva was feeling so much better this morning that she wanted to come to the table for breakfast."

"That's great." I tried to sound as if I really meant it even though I didn't. I'd planned to somehow say something to Mom this morning to make up for the things I hadn't said last night, but I couldn't talk with Aunt Reva sitting there watching me. She always seemed to be watching me.

Mom hugged me and said, "You look especially pretty this morning, Alyssa. That color almost makes your eyes look blue."

Remembering my wish from the night before, I felt funny as I said, "Not really."

"Millicent's eyes were blue." Aunt Reva's eyes fastened on me. "But not as blue as mine."

I pulled my eyes away from hers. "My eyes are gray."

"And pretty gray eyes, too," Mom said. She was trying her best to clear the odd tension that had sprung up between Aunt Reva and me.

"Gray eyes are fine unless you wish for blue ones." Aunt Reva was still staring at me. "I'll bet you wish you had blue eyes."

"Not really," I said and dropped a kiss on Mom's cheek before I ran out to the truck.

As I was getting out at school, Dad told me I should go straight home after school to stay with Aunt Reva while Mom went to the doctor. "You don't mind, do you, Lyssie?"

"No," I lied. "I don't mind."

I slammed the truck door behind me and ran on into the school. I didn't want to stay with Aunt Reva, but I wasn't about to let my dread of the afternoon ruin my whole day. I wouldn't think about any of it now. Not crazy old Aunt Reva, or Mom having a baby, or Dad and I not being able to talk, really talk.

There'd be plenty of time to worry about all that later while I sat with Aunt Reva.

Chapter 5

When I spotted Marci and Doug Clifton coming in the side door from the parking lot, I couldn't keep from smiling at the little surge of disappointment I felt. My "magic mirror" hadn't been able to deliver my morning's wish.

Marci saw me and waved for me to wait for her. As I waited, I shifted from one foot to the other there in the middle of the kids swarming around me and worried about what I'd say to Doug Clifton, who was following Marci across the lobby.

"It's a madhouse in here," Marci said a little breathlessly. "And we're late as usual."

Doug laughed. "And whose fault is that?" He looked at me and my knees went weak. "Marci has to try on fifteen outfits before she can decide what to wear."

Marci slapped his arm. "I do not, and anyway even if I did, I'd still have to wait on you. You take hours just combing your hair." She looked over at me as if to get my sympathy. "And they say girls are vain."

As we moved toward our lockers, Doug started along with us, and Marci gave him a funny look. "Your locker isn't this way," she said.

"No," he agreed.

"You'll be late for class."

"I've got plenty of time." She gave him another

funny look, and he sort of smiled and said, "I was just trying to give you a chance to remember your manners and introduce me to your friend."

"I told you about Alyssa."

"But you didn't introduce us." His clear blue eyes were totally on me. "Hi, Alyssa. I'm Doug Clifton."

"I know," I stammered.

His smile was slow, but friendly and definitely interested. "I guess Marci told you all about me, too."

"Just that you liked to sing." I tried to sound friendly without sounding flirty. No matter what I'd wished that morning in my mirror, I didn't really want to steal Marci's boyfriend. I almost grinned at the thought. Imagine me stealing any boy away from Marci. Millicent's mirror must be affecting my brain.

"Good. She sometimes forgets to say nice things about me," he said.

"Oh, for heaven's sake," Marci said as she started working the combination of her locker. "You're going to make us all late, Doug."

"See you later then, Alyssa," Doug said as he turned back up the hall.

"Sure," I said, turning to my own locker but without the slightest idea what numbers I needed to open the combination.

"Brothers," Marci muttered as she pulled open her locker. "Do you have any?"

"Any what?" I said as I dredged up the numbers of my combination.

"Brothers. I mean I love Doug, but sometimes he can be a real pain. Imagine hitting on you with a line like that."

I took my time changing my books as I ran her words through my head. "You mean Doug's your brother?"

"Of course he is." Marci looked at me. "Didn't you know that?"

"Your names aren't the same."

"Same mother, different fathers. What did you think he was?"

"I don't know," I said as I softly shut my locker. "We'd better hurry. It's almost time for the bell."

"You thought he was my boyfriend." Marci burst out laughing. "No wonder you looked so funny when he started hitting on you."

I didn't laugh.

Marci tried to choke back her own laughter. "I'm sorry, Alyssa. I guess it's not funny, but if you could have seen your face. I'll bet Doug's still wondering what he said that made you turn so pale. I thought there for a minute you were going to faint, and while Doug's used to girls liking him, he's never made one actually faint before."

"I feel like such a nut," I said, my face flaming now.

"No, no." Marci squeezed my arm. "If you really like Doug, it might be the best thing. Most girls are just all too easy to read when it comes to Doug. Maybe it's better to keep him guessing."

There wasn't time to say any more as we slipped into our first class just seconds ahead of the bell.

I tried to listen to Mrs. Lunsford as she began lecturing us about one-cell life forms. I really did, but my mind was miles away from biology. It was back in my room with Millicent's mirror.

"We can unravel the mysteries of life only by studying the simplest life forms," Mrs. Lunsford was saying.

I quit listening again. There was no way that my wish in the mirror had anything to do with Marci and

44

Doug being sister and brother. They'd always been sister and brother. I just hadn't known it.

Still, I wondered if I should put the mirror back in the attic, because Marci had been right. I had felt faint when I realized Doug was flirting with me, but it'd had nothing to do with the way I'd felt about him. I hadn't been able to think of anything except that the mirror was granting another wish.

I shook myself a little and tried harder to listen to Mrs. Lunsford. I repeated her every word silently in my mind after she said it. But the mirror was still flashing all around my thoughts, and I could hardly keep from turning to the boy behind me and asking him what color my eyes were.

When I got home from school, Mom was waiting at the door. "You shouldn't have any problems," she said as she gave me a kiss. "She's usually very quiet this time of the day, and Robbie's at the store with your father."

"All right."

Mom hesitated, then said, "Thanks for being such a sweetheart, honey. I know you don't like to sit with Aunt Reva."

"It's okay. I don't really mind."

After Mom left, I ran upstairs to change clothes. I left my door open so that I could hear Aunt Reva if she called.

Before I went back downstairs I took a quick look in the mirror. My eyes were definitely gray now that I was no longer wearing the blue blouse. Still, Doug wasn't Marci's boyfriend.

He wasn't mine either, I reminded myself as I ran back down the steps. It was silly for me to even think he might be in spite of the way he'd talked to me that morning.

I hadn't talked to him again. Marci and I had eaten

lunch together, but she'd been too busy telling me about this running argument she and her mother were having to say anything about Doug.

"No matter what I do, I can't please her," Marci had said.

I'd tried to sympathize with her, but I kept wanting to ask her if she really thought Doug could be interested in me, plain Alyssa Blake.

I didn't see Doug again until chorus, but even there I didn't get a chance to talk to him. Mr. Birdsong had us singing nonstop from bell to bell. He didn't stop once to correct sour notes or try for improvement. We just sang through one song after another while he hopped around in front of us, seeming to enjoy himself immensely.

I had dared a few looks over at Doug and flushed when once I caught his eyes on me.

After class I'd had to rush out to catch the bus home. There hadn't been time to talk to him, and even if there had, I wouldn't have known what to say. If I got a chance, I'd ask Marci. She'd know what to say to make a boy think you were cute, because even if Doug was her brother and not a boyfriend, she had plenty of others. Me, I only dreamed and wished I had boyfriends.

With a last quick look at the mirror, I went back downstairs. All was still quiet from Aunt Reva's room. I hesitated at the bottom of the steps, wondering if I should go in and check on her, but if she was napping, I didn't want to disturb her.

As I went on into the kitchen to get something to eat, I sang a silly little song about wishing that I'd made up years ago.

"Lyssie wishes wishes would come true. Lyssie wishes wishes for you. What wishes will Lyssie wish?"

I pulled an apple out of the bottom of the refrigerator and smiled, remembering that it had been Dad who had made up the song as a game we could play when business was slow at the fruit stand. I laughed aloud when I thought of some of the crazy things we'd dreamed up to wish. That was when Dad had first started calling me Lyssie the wisher.

I wished I could be down at the fruit stand now sorting through oranges and cauliflower heads instead of here in this quiet old house.

That had been the first thing I'd noticed about the house after we'd moved in. How quiet it was.

I tried to sing another song, but the words just sort of died in the air. I gave it up and went into the living room to wait out the hours till Mom came back from the doctor. The house was different with Mom there. I hardly ever noticed the silence then.

"Vivien." Aunt Reva's voice broke into the silence. "Vivien."

Before I could get to her door, she'd already called five times.

"Mom's not here. Do you need something?"

Aunt Reva scowled at me from her bed. "I wouldn't have called if I hadn't needed something. Where is your mother?"

"She had to go out." I inched closer to the bed. "Do you want a drink of water or something?"

"I want to get up." She threw off the quilt she'd had over her legs. "Well, don't just stand there. Come help me."

I put my arm around her and helped pull her to a sitting position. Her peculiar odor of bed, powder, and age filled my head, but I kept a smile on my face even while my wishing song was echoing through my mind. Let Lyssie wish. Lyssie wishes she were anywhere but here.

When Aunt Reva was sitting up on the side of the bed, I placed her walker directly in front of her. "Do you want to go into the living room?"

"I don't want to sit here all day." She struggled to her feet. "Where is Vivien?"

"She had to go to town," I said.

Aunt Reva placed the walker away from her and then slowly moved her feet forward. Each time she moved the walker it thudded heavily against the floor. I walked along behind her, not sure if I should be ready to catch her if she fell or what. I was relieved when she was settled in her chair in the living room.

"Do you want me to get you something, turn on the television, or anything?" I asked.

"No, there's nothing on television except nonsense anyway. I don't know why anybody ever watches it."

It promised to be a long hour. I picked up my book and pretended to read in hopes she wouldn't want to talk.

It didn't work. "I know where Vivien is," she said.

I looked up, but didn't say anything.

"She's gone to the doctor," Aunt Reva said smugly as though she knew something she wasn't supposed to know. "She ought to be ashamed, getting in the family way at her age. She and Hewitt should have known better."

I decided silence might be the best answer. She, too, lapsed into silence for so long that I hoped she'd gone back to sleep, but when I chanced a look up from my page, she was watching me.

"Did you want something?" I asked with a side-long glance at the clock. Mom had been gone forty-three minutes.

"No."

"Okay." I looked back down at my book. "If you do, let me know."

The silence fell over us once more as I tried to start reading again, but the words just floated on the pages in front of me in a strange, disjointed way. None of them made any sense. Still, I kept my eyes on the page, because I knew if I looked up I'd see her staring at me.

"You don't want to have a sister, do you?" she said after what seemed like an hour, but really was only six minutes when I looked at the clock.

"The baby might be a boy, and anyway I'd just as soon have a sister as another brother. It wouldn't make any difference to me."

"You don't want either one."

"Mom and Dad do." I looked back down at my book.

"You're selfish," Aunt Reva said. "Just like Millicent."

I looked back up at her at the mention of Millicent.

She almost smiled. "That got your attention, didn't it? You want to know about Millicent, don't you?"

She was right. I did want to know about Millicent, but I didn't know why. "Did you not want a sister before Millicent was born?" I asked.

"It was her that didn't want a sister. She was the oldest."

"Oh." I remembered the picture I'd found in the attic. I'd thought Millicent was the youngest.

Aunt Reva's eyes wandered away from me, and for a few minutes I thought she wasn't going to say anything else. Then she went on. "There were only thirteen months between us. My mother was sickly while she carried me, and they had to feed Millicent with a bottle."

"Lots of babies are fed with bottles."

"Not then they weren't. It was unnatural. Millicent thought it was my fault, as though I could have kept

49

from being born. She was selfish.'' Aunt Reva's eyes came back to me. ''You're selfish, too. Always hiding away up in your room, thinking about yourself, looking in Millicent's mirror.''

''I'm not in my room now,'' I said, trying to stay calm.

''But you want to be.''

I couldn't deny that, so I just turned my eyes away from her back to the clock. I thought maybe I could somehow will the hands to move faster, but they seemed to be stuck in the same spot. I got up and said, ''Maybe I should start some supper for Mom.''

''I thought you wanted to know about Millicent.''

''I know enough about her,'' I said.

''And her mirror?''

''What about the mirror? It's just a mirror, isn't it?''

''Millicent didn't think so. She used to cover it up with a black cloth when she left her room because she didn't want anybody else to look in it.''

''It sounds like Millicent had problems.''

''Yes. She was selfish like you.''

''I don't care if anybody looks in the mirror.''

''Then maybe you should,'' Aunt Reva said mysteriously. ''Maybe you should.''

I started to go on to the kitchen. She was just trying to make me feel funny. The problem was it was working, because I did feel funny, even a little uneasy when I thought about the mirror.

I looked back at Aunt Reva. Her head was drooping. ''Why?'' I asked suddenly. She looked up at me with a bewildered look. ''Why should I keep anybody else from looking in the mirror? What's wrong with it?''

She frowned at me. ''Young people, always pestering you with silly questions.''

"You're the one who started talking about it."

"About what?"

"Millicent's mirror. You said there was something strange about it."

"I didn't say that." She rubbed her forehead with her hand. "My head hurts. Get me my medicine."

I gave her the medicine and then stayed out in the kitchen till after Mom got home. Mom asked me if everything had gone all right, and I lied and said yes. I asked her if everything had gone all right at the doctor, and she said yes.

Then Dad and Robbie came in, and the spooky silence of the old house vanished. It was just an old house again and Aunt Reva just an old woman. And when I went up to my room after supper, Millicent's mirror was just a mirror.

I made myself remember that the next morning as I got ready for school. I wouldn't let myself wish for anything. I just combed my hair and smoothed on my makeup while I worried about what I would say if Doug talked to me at school.

As I was leaving my room, I looked back and imagined the mirror hidden by a black cloth. Why would she cover it up?

And in spite of myself as I hesitated there at the door, I wanted to go back and touch the glass and make a wish just to see. Just in case it worked.

What would I wish for if I were going to let myself wish? Something sensible for a change. Maybe for voice lessons. Still it might be better to stick with something that had a chance of coming true. I could wish Doug Clifton would talk to me again and that I would think of something witty and charming to say.

But why be practical? Why not wish for something so crazy that it was impossible? Like Aunt Reva laughing. It had to have been years since she'd

51

laughed. Years. Or that I'd meet someone famous. That would surely be impossible here in Brookdale.

I smiled as I turned away from the mirror. That ought to be enough wishes to keep even the most magical mirror busy for a while.

Chapter 6

Doug did talk to me that day, and I didn't have any trouble at all knowing what to say to him. It came almost naturally, as if just hanging around with Marci had somehow given me her ease at making friends.

"You really like Doug, don't you?" Marci said while we were eating lunch.

"He's cute," I admitted.

"Yeah, my brother, every girl's wish come true. Good looking, nice body, fantastic eyes, and a great personality."

"Don't you like him?"

"Of course I do. He's a great guy like I said. It's just that, well, I wouldn't want him to mess up what promises to be a great friendship between us, Alyssa."

"What do you mean?"

"Well, say things didn't work out between you and Doug. Then you might get mad at me, too." Marci looked at me over her milk. "I'd hate for that to happen, because I think we could be great friends. I mean, I can talk to you, and I feel like you understand. We're so much alike."

"Alike?" I couldn't keep the surprise out of my voice.

"Don't you think so? We're the same age. We both sing. We both laugh at the same things. We're both fairly attractive girls. I mean, I think I am in spite of what Mother says.''

''You're better than attractive, Marci. You're really pretty. Me, I'm average, ordinary.''

''You're a special kind of pretty, Alyssa. Maybe it doesn't shine through all the time, but when you sing, then you radiate.''

''You sound like my dad. He's always trying to sound poetic when he describes someone.''

''My daddy's anything but poetic. He'd say poetry doesn't pay.''

''He'd be right about that.''

Marci set down her milk carton. ''How would you know?''

I shrugged a little. ''My father sometimes tries to sell the poems he writes.''

Marci's eyes took on a new sparkle. ''Your father writes poetry?''

''Sometimes.''

''Gee, that must be great, having a father who writes poetry.''

''You might not think it was so wonderful if it was your father.''

''Why not?''

''We don't have a maid.''

''Celina?'' Marci waved her hand as if having a maid was nothing. ''She's practically like one of the family, and we really couldn't get by without her. Mother was in the entertainment business, and she never really learned how to cook or anything.''

''The entertainment business?'' Now it was my turn to get shiny eyes. ''What did she do?''

''She sang. Marcella Devine.'' Marci drew out the letters of the name in the air. ''Daddy says she was famous, and I guess she was, because she did shows in Las Vegas and even had a couple of *Billboard* hits.

Of course all that was a long time ago, before she married my father and they decided to settle in Brookdale. Heaven only knows why. She said she was tired of being in the spotlight, but Brookdale? I mean she could have retired from the bright lights in San Francisco or New Orleans. Some place, any place more exciting than here.''

I couldn't stop staring at Marci. "I sometimes wish I could be a singer,'' I finally said. At the word *wish*, a funny, uneasy feeling began growing in the pit of my stomach. I pushed it away. I wouldn't think about Millicent's mirror. It had nothing to do with Marci's mother having once sung on the stage in Las Vegas.

"My mother says it's a hard life. There's so much pressure on you to keep making hits. She says she's glad she's out of it, but at the same time she keeps pushing me like she thinks she can force my voice to match hers. I mean, I like to sing, but I'll never be good enough to make records. Besides, I don't even want to.''

"What do you want to do?''

"I don't know. Maybe be a journalist.''

"A journalist?''

Marci sighed and piled her napkin and milk carton on her tray. "That's just how my mother says it.''

"I'm sorry,'' I said quickly as I picked up my tray and followed her away from the table. "I didn't mean that the way it sounded. I was just surprised.''

"It's okay.'' Marci placed her tray carefully on top of the others piled in the window. "I'm used to it. When you're pretty, nobody ever takes you seriously.'' She waited for me before she started out to the hall. "What do your parents want you to do?''

"I don't know. I guess they're leaving that up to me.''

"Sounds like heaven," Marci said. "You don't know how lucky you are."

"I guess not," I said.

Marci laughed. "That's what Mother's always telling me. 'You don't know how lucky you are.'" Marci lowered her voice dramatically. Then she shook her head and added, "I can't believe I'm telling you the same thing."

"And I can't believe your mother was a famous singer."

Marci grinned at me. "Would you like to meet the one and only Marcella Devine?"

"Well, sure. That would be great."

"Then why don't you come home with me this afternoon? You might even get to flirt with Doug a little more. I mean, you will promise to still be my friend even if you do fall for Doug, won't you? And then tomorrow or whenever I can come over to your house."

The bell rang, and I didn't have time to do anything but nod.

I didn't see Marci again until chorus, where Mr. Birdsong had a whole new bunch of songs for us to sing through. We had yet to learn any one song, but we must have sung through hundreds. I was beginning to see why the kids at Brookdale High thought chorus was a joke.

"Very good," Mr. Birdsong said, stopping us in mid-song when the bell rang. Then, as everybody made a dash for the door, he yelled over the commotion, "Lisa Blake, could you stay a moment after class?"

Marci whispered that she and Doug would wait for me. "I don't know what Birdie could want," she said. "He's never kept anybody after class before."

Mr. Birdsong waited till all the other kids had filed

56

out before he looked at me and said, "Would you like to learn to sing better, Alison? Develop your voice and learn to breathe correctly?"

"Of course. I practice all I can," I said.

"But you need guidance. Someone to help you develop your potential."

"I can't afford lessons."

"No, no," he said, throwing his hands up. "I'll be your singing coach. Not for money. For results."

"Why?"

"Because you are in need of a teacher, and I am in need of a pupil. Do you agree?"

"I guess so."

"Good. You come to the school at ten o'clock Saturday morning, and we will have a lesson." He held out his hand which I finally realized he meant me to shake. "I will be a demanding teacher, but you will do well."

A demanding teacher? Mr. Birdsong? As I went out into the hall, I felt a little dizzy. Maybe I was still dreaming. Maybe none of this was really happening. Maybe I shouldn't have looked back at Millicent's mirror and thought up those crazy wishes.

Doug and Marci were waiting for me in the hall. "What did he want?" Marci asked.

"He wants to give me voice lessons."

"Birdie? How did you get out of that one?" Marci asked, and then her smile faded when I just sort of shrugged. "You didn't tell him you'd do it, did you?"

"Why not?" I asked.

"Birdie?" This time her voice was even more incredulous. "What in the world could he teach you?"

"I don't know." I was beginning to feel silly.

"Lay off, Marci," Doug said. "Old Birdie's not that bad."

I glanced up at Doug in gratitude while I felt a

57

surge of expectation inside me. I'd wanted voice lessons. I'd even wished for voice lessons. Now I was going to get them, and I wanted to believe they'd help me. But when I looked back at Marci, her face was still skeptical, so I just said, "It can't hurt anything if Mom and Dad will let me."

"I wish you'd take lessons from Mr. Wilson with me. Mother says he's the best in the area."

"There's no need wishing for the impossible," I said and then almost stopped in my tracks. Maybe if I'd wished for lessons from Mr. Wilson that morning, then that's what I'd have now instead of lessons from Mr. Birdsong.

I lagged a little behind Marci. Doug dropped back a couple of steps to walk beside me.

"Don't let Marci upset you, Alyssa," he said softly. "She just gets carried away by her own plans sometimes. Actually Birdie probably knows as much about music as anybody around here. He can't help it if he's a little weird in the head."

I laughed, and Marci looked back at us. "A private joke?" she asked with raised eyebrows.

"Could be," Doug said with a grin before he fished his car keys out of his pocket and loped off across the parking lot to get his car.

Dressed in a flowing silk lounging robe, Marcella Devine Reid was everything I expected and more. Her blonde hair was carefully styled, her nails manicured, and if there was a flaw in her beauty, I couldn't spot it through her makeup. She looked like she was just waiting for the moment when she would step out onto the stage.

After the introductions, she said something about how nice it was to meet one of Marci's little friends, and I embarrassed myself by saying, "Are you singing somewhere tonight?"

Marci started to say something, but Mrs. Reid laughed first. Her laugh had a musical sound and yet at the same time a note that jarred. Out of the corner of my eye, I saw Doug slip out of the room. I wasn't sure why what I'd said was so wrong. I just knew it was, and my face flamed.

"Oh, my dear child, I don't sing in public anymore," she said in a low, husky voice. She smiled over at Marci before she went on. "Marci will be the next star in the family."

"Mother, don't start that," Marci said without smiling. "You know I'm not going to be a singer, but Alyssa says she might. She has a beautiful voice."

"Really? How nice." Mrs. Reid's eyes came back to me, then as quickly darted away to the clock in the stark white case on the mantel.

I followed her glance and noticed for the first time that everything in the room was white or black except the ruby red of the throw pillows on the couch. Her robe was the exact same red.

I stood there awkwardly as the quiet grew, afraid to open my mouth for fear that I'd say the wrong thing again. Marci came to my rescue by touching my arm and saying, "Let's go out to the kitchen and find something to eat."

Although the kitchen was huge, with a stainless steel work area in the middle of it, it still had more of a feeling of home than the living room had had.

A little woman wearing a black uniform with a white apron turned to smile at me. "It is good to meet Marci's friend," she said.

"This is Celina," Marci said. "Our treasure, the best cook in the state."

Celina's smile got even brighter. "I'll fix you snacking food."

Doug, who was leaning on the counter already halfway through a sandwich, looked at me with an odd little grin. "Dismissed from the great presence already?"

"She's beautiful," I stammered. "I'd love to hear her sing."

"She doesn't anymore," Marci said as she took a couple of glasses out of the cabinet.

"Ever? Not even for fun?"

Marci shook her head. "She says it strains her voice too much."

Doug pushed away from the counter. "We still have some of her records around here somewhere. You can listen to one of them, Alyssa, if you want to hear her sing."

"Oh, don't get that old thing out," Marci said, but Doug had already left the kitchen. Marci made a face as she handed me a soft drink out of the refrigerator.

Doug came back with a forty-five record which he held out to me. "Marcella Devine's biggest hit. 'Always and Forever.'"

I held the record with a feeling of awe. I had just met the woman whose voice was on this record, and I wondered how it would feel to be holding a record with my own name on the label.

"If you want to hear it, we can go up to my room," Doug was saying.

Marci broke in before I could answer. "I don't want to hear it."

"But maybe Alyssa does," Doug said.

They glared at each other for a minute, and I began to wish I'd gone to Dad's fruit stand after school. I started to hand the record back to Doug. "I can listen to it another time," I said.

"Take it home with you," Doug insisted. "You can listen to it and then bring it back. I know you're curious to hear what Marcella Devine sounded like in her prime."

Marci caught the sound of the rhyme and laughed. "Marcella Devine in her prime," she repeated.

After that my visit went smoother. When we'd finished off Celina's cookies, Doug went off to play ball with some buddies, but he made a point of telling me goodbye first. Then Marci took me upstairs to see her room and let me peek at Doug's before we went out back and settled in lounge chairs around the pool.

I felt sort of like I was in a dream as I listened to Marci talk and watched the sunlight bounce off the pool water. Of course I'd known people lived like this, but it was different sitting here being almost a part of it all.

Later I carried the record home and wondered what I'd tell Doug the next day when I took it back. I hadn't had the nerve to tell him our only record player had gotten broken in the move to Aunt Reva's house.

Chapter 7

I couldn't wait to tell Mom about Marci's house and her celebrity mother, so as soon as I got home I carried the record out to the sun porch where Mom was working and Aunt Reva was napping in the sun.

Pegs that had once held coats and hats now held coils of white oak and walnut bark, while above our heads a dozen finished baskets hung from nails Dad had driven in the porch rafters. Organized clutter covered Mom's worktable.

Mom had the peaceful, contented look on her face that she always had when she was weaving her baskets, but today there was something more in her face that made me know she was thinking about the baby forming inside her. I just couldn't understand how she could be so happy about having a baby. Even if she wasn't too old and even if it wasn't dangerous for her, we still needed everything but a baby around here. For the first time I wondered what Marci would think when she found out.

Mom looked up from her basket and noticed me there in the doorway. "Alyssa. I was beginning to get worried about you."

"I've been at Marci's house." Then remembering how Marcella Devine had looked in her black and white living room, I forgot all my worries about the baby and began trying to tell Mom everything. My words spilled out end over end as I jumped from one wonder to the next.

Mom listened patiently and then said, "It sounds like a lovely house. Imagine. A big kitchen like that to work in."

"Mrs. Reid doesn't do any of the work. They have a maid for that. Her name's Celina, and she must be foreign because she has a funny accent."

"What does she do then? This Reid woman." Aunt Reva raised her chin up from her chest to stare at me.

"I don't know. Whatever she wants to, I guess."

"She just sits there and lets people wait on her like me," Aunt Reva said. "Totally useless."

"Now Aunt Reva," Mom started.

"It's the truth, Vivien, but I've got an excuse. I'm old. What's her excuse?"

Aunt Reva's eyes bored into me, demanding an answer. I waited for Mom to say something to help me out, but she only smiled a little as she shaped another basket rib.

So I said, "Mrs. Reid used to be a singer. Marci said she was famous, that she sang on the stage out in Las Vegas."

"Well, that explains it then," Aunt Reva said, and when Mom laughed, I could have sworn that Aunt Reva almost smiled.

I held up the record. "This was one of her hits. 'Always and Forever.' "

Mom kept shaping the basket, but she read the label on the record when I held it out to her. "Marcella Devine. I don't remember the name, but I remember the song. 'Always, forever, my love,' " Mom sang the last few words.

"Do you remember the rest of it?" I asked.

Mom thought a minute before she said, "I'm afraid I don't, Alyssa. That was so long ago."

"How long ago?" I asked.

"I must have been your age, maybe a little older." Mom stopped working on the basket for a moment and looked out toward the sky. "When I think about that time now and remember some of the things I did, it almost seems like I'm thinking about a different person and not myself at all." Her eyes came back to me and then Aunt Reva. "Is that the way it is with you, too, Aunt Reva?"

"Sometimes. Other times I feel like I'm still that young girl and this helpless heap here is the person I don't know." She pointed at herself.

I looked from the record to Aunt Reva. How could she feel young?

"What is it about being a teenager that is so special?" Mom said as she went back to working her basket reeds.

"Or so bad." Aunt Reva let her chin sink back down on her chest.

I looked at the record again. "I wish I knew how it sounded."

"Why don't you play it?" Mom asked.

"I can't. Don't you remember? The record player broke when we moved."

A strange sound came from Aunt Reva, like the sound of rusty iron joints beginning to move. "Now that is a fix. A record and no record player." Again she made the strange noise.

Dad came out on the porch. "Here you are," he said. "All my lovely ladies in one room. What's so funny anyway?"

Aunt Reva looked up and said, "You'll have to ask your girl that."

Dad glanced over at me, but I was staring at Aunt Reva. "Funny?" I whispered.

64

"How was your day at the store?" Mom was saying as Dad leaned over to kiss her.

Dad sang his answer in a silly voice. "I sold a few oranges and lots of apples, but even more bananas in little yellow wrapples."

"Oh, Hewitt, are you ever going to grow up?" Aunt Reva said, and then the odd noise rumbled out of her again. This time there could be no doubt.

"You are laughing," I said, my eyes riveted to her face. "I didn't think you ever laughed."

"Alyssa," Dad said sternly, but I barely heard him.

Aunt Reva met my stare and knew at once. "You wished it, didn't you? You wished that I would laugh."

The rest of the room faded away as the old woman and I looked at each other. Somewhere in the background Dad was saying, "That was sweet of you, Lyssie. Making a wish for Aunt Reva."

"Nothing sweet about it, was there, girl?" Aunt Reva said.

"I didn't think you'd laugh."

"Break it, girl. Now. Before it's too late."

"What are you two talking about?" Dad asked. "Break what?"

"The girl knows." Aunt Reva dropped her eyes to her hands.

Mom and Dad looked at me, waiting for me to explain while I suddenly felt as though something was separating me from them. I had to try twice before I could say anything at all. "The record player," I finally got out. "It's broken and I can't play this record Marci's mother made."

I looked at Aunt Reva out of the corner of my eye, but she didn't raise her head to look at me. Though I rushed on telling Dad about Marcella Devine, the excitement I'd felt earlier had disappeared, and the words were just curtains I was pulling over what was really going through my mind.

I quit talking when all the words were finally gone. Dad looked at the record and sang the same part of the song Mom had sung.

"That's all I could remember, too." Mom laughed.

I was glad when Robbie came bounding in the back door, knocking over baskets as he piled through us to Mom. "I saw a blue bird. I saw a bright blue bird. He's right out there in the tree."

Everything else was forgotten then as Mom and Dad followed Robbie back outside to see the bird. I didn't go with them. Instead I picked up the record off Mom's worktable and headed for the stairs. As I passed close to Aunt Reva, she reached out a hand and clutched my arm.

"It's wicked," she said.

I tried to pull away from her, but she hung onto my arm that much tighter. "I don't know what you're talking about."

"You know. You wished I would laugh, didn't you?"

I yanked my arm free. "It was just a silly thought. It didn't mean anything."

"You asked it to happen." She reached toward me again, but I backed away from her. Her voice fell to a whisper. "Be careful what you wish, what you even think."

I started to run from the room, but I stopped before I reached the door. "What happened to Millicent?"

"I told you. She died," Aunt Reva said without looking up.

"Because of the mirror?"

She still didn't look up, and I could barely hear her answer. "No, because of me."

"What do you mean?"

But she wouldn't explain. "Break it before it's too late."

I ran from her then, all the way up the steps and into my room as though her words were pursuing me.

I tried to keep my eyes away from the mirror, but it was as if the mirror were the only thing in the room. I could look no place else.

I stared at my reflection without seeing what I looked like now. Instead I saw myself as I had been that morning looking back, making my silly, impossible wishes. Voice lessons, meeting someone famous, and most impossible of all, Aunt Reva laughing. We'd been here for weeks, and she'd never even smiled, much less laughed. Why had she picked today to laugh?

"Break it," she'd said. "It's wicked."

I picked up the stool that was in front of the table under the mirror, but when I raised it, I caught full sight of myself in the mirror. I stood poised there for a long moment. Then, carefully, I set the stool back on the floor so softly that the legs made no noise when they touched the wooden floor.

I stared at myself in the mirror until my eyes and nose and mouth almost seemed to melt together. Lyssie the wisher.

I'd quit wishing. It was that simple. Not that I believed the mirror had any powers, but if I didn't make wishes then they couldn't come true.

The decision made, I nodded at the girl in the mirror, and she nodded back at me. I was too old now for wishing anyway. Things didn't happen just because you wished they would.

I half-smiled at the thought. I was telling myself to stop wishing not because my wishes hadn't come true but because they had. The girl in the mirror smiled back at me.

Why did I have the crazy feeling all at once that the girl in the mirror wasn't me? Didn't look like me. But that was silly. I turned away from the mirror and then back. There I was. Of course it was me. I was letting Aunt Reva put weird ideas about the mirror into my head.

The glass on the mirror sparkled and sent back my smile truly this time.

When I turned away from the mirror, my eyes fell on the record I'd laid on top of my books. I wished I had a way to play it.

The thought brought me up short, and I sneaked a look over my shoulder at the mirror. It caught light from somewhere and threw it back at me.

"It's just a mirror," I muttered to myself, turning back around. I picked up the record. Wishing I had a way to play it was only a thought, not a real wish. Still, the thought had made me realize that it wasn't going to be easy to stop wishing completely.

I'd always wished for things whether I expected to get them or not. Wishing was a game of pretend, a gateway to fantasy.

I used to wish I was a princess who lived in a castle and sang songs to the wind out of a turret window. All that was fun, but I hadn't really wanted it to be true. What would happen if I wished that now? Would this old house groan and shake and stretch into a castle? The thought was so silly that I laughed. No mirror was that magical.

No mirror was magical at all. I was just letting Aunt Reva's superstitions infect me.

Still, I felt oddly uneasy with the mirror sparkling behind me. Magical or not, there was something different about it, and something about Aunt Reva that was different. Or maybe it was Millicent who had been different. Why wouldn't Aunt Reva tell me what had happened to Millicent? And what could she have meant when she'd said she had caused her to die?

All I had to do was wish I knew. The idea seemed to come unbidden to my mind. I could just turn around, look into the mirror, and wish I knew what had happened to Millicent, and I would.

I fought the desire to try it. I wasn't going to make any more wishes. I'd already decided.

If I found out what happened to Millicent it would have to be a different way. Still, the sparkle of the mirror pulled at my eyes until I couldn't stand it. I grabbed my sweater off the end of the bed and draped it over the glass, looping the sleeves behind the frame, but the glitter of the mirror escaped around the edges of the sweater.

I slipped out of my room, and almost without realizing what I was doing, I climbed the stairs to the attic.

Going straight to the trunk, I pulled out the clothes and found the picture. It was just like I remembered. One girl pretty, one girl plain. Neither girl smiling. Both in black.

I stuffed the dresses back into the trunk. I'd be able to see the faces in the picture better downstairs since the light was fading rapidly up here.

Dad was in the hallway when I came back down the attic steps. "Oh, there you are, Lyssie. I was just coming up to get you." Dad gave me a funny look. "What were you doing up in the attic? Have you got your diary hidden up there?"

"I don't have a diary," I said while the picture burned into my hand. We'd been told not to bother Aunt Reva's things.

"Everybody should keep a diary," Dad said. "At least for a few days."

"Did you?" I held the picture close against me as I started down the hall.

"Of course. I wrote a poem in it every day. Bad poems mostly, but that's the good thing about a diary. Nobody ever has to see it but you."

"Do you suppose Aunt Reva ever kept a diary?" I asked suddenly, even more aware of the picture in my hand and hoping more than ever that Dad wouldn't notice it.

"Maybe," Dad said. "What have you got there?"

"Just an old picture I came across while I was up there looking around." I reluctantly held it out to Dad. "Do you think one of those girls is Aunt Reva?"

"Could be." Dad stared at the picture.

I pointed to the smaller girl. "She's pretty, isn't she?"

"She has a certain youthful beauty." Dad smiled up at me. "The same as you."

"Oh, Dad, don't be silly, but do you think that could be the Millicent Aunt Reva's always talking about? The one she said owned the mirror."

"I don't know. Why don't you take the picture down and ask her?"

"I can't," I said as I took the picture back. "She might be mad if she knew I'd been into her things up in the attic, and I wouldn't want to upset her."

"Maybe you're right. She was pretty firm about you and Robbie staying out of her things."

"I didn't hurt anything. I was just looking around."

"For an old record player, I'll bet," Dad said with a grin. "That's why I came upstairs to get you. I fixed the record player. So get that record, and we'll all listen to it. And you say you really met the woman who recorded it?"

I laid the picture on the table under the mirror. The

mirror looked ridiculous with my sweater tied around it, but I didn't take it off. I didn't dare.

I picked up the record and ran downstairs where the family was waiting.

Chapter 8

We listened to the record three times. By the last play through Mom and Dad were singing every word along with Marcella Devine. While I didn't especially like the song, the voice was unmistakably Marci's mother, and that was enough to give me goosebumps. I actually knew the person singing on that record.

I watched the black disc spin around and around. How would it feel to have your own record? I almost wished I knew, but caught myself in time. Of course a wish downstairs surely wouldn't be captured by the mirror upstairs.

To keep from thinking about the mirror, I began listening to the voice on the record even more intently.

When the last notes of the music faded away, Mom and Dad laughed, joined by some memory out of the past that the song had awakened inside them. "That was fun," Dad said as he turned the record over and put it back on the turntable. "Let's see what's on the other side."

"I think we've had enough of this nonsense," Aunt Reva said. "It's time for supper."

"In a minute, Aunt Reva," Mom said. "It won't take long to listen to the other side of the record, and don't you think it's exciting that the singer lives right here in Brookdale?"

72

"I never met her," Aunt Reva said.

"But Alyssa did," Dad said. "She's been hobnobbing with the rich and famous."

Remembering my silly wish to meet someone famous, I blushed scarlet. I stared at the record and hoped nobody would notice, but I could almost feel Aunt Reva's eyes boring into me.

Marcella Devine sang "Blue Tomorrow" in the same low, husky voice as she'd sung "Always and Forever," but something was missing. The sound was almost flat.

"The flip sides of forty-fives were always throwaways," Dad said when the song ended. "They were songs nobody expected to be popular."

"They didn't want you to be able to buy two hits for the price of one record," Mom said as Dad took the record off the turntable. "I used to have more than a hundred records like that. I might even have had that one."

"A hundred records?" I looked at her in surprise. I didn't own one hit record. Not one. "What happened to them all?"

Mom stood up and ran her hands across her stomach. "I don't know. I suppose my brother got rid of them after my father died."

"I didn't know you had a brother," I said, my surprise growing.

Mom was standing absolutely still, staring a bit to one side of my face. "Well, we can't know everything about one another."

"But your brother. That would be my uncle."

Mom's face softened a bit. "He was quite a bit older than me, and we didn't get on, Alyssa. I haven't seen him for years."

I looked over at Robbie running his toy cars around the bricks on the fireplace.

73

Mom followed my look. "It won't be that way for you and Robbie or even this new one on the way. You'll always be close because you'll love one another."

Aunt Reva looked up. "Just being sisters and brothers doesn't guarantee you'll love one another."

"I love Robbie," I said quickly. "Even if he is a pest sometimes."

"Of course you do, Alyssa," Mom said. "But it was different for me. After my mother died, Arthur and I just didn't have much of a chance. He was always away at school, and then so was I. We only saw each other on holidays."

Dad was twirling the record in his hands, watching Mom uneasily. I felt strange as I realized for the first time how much I didn't know about them. They'd always just been there, steady and dependable. I'd never thought about them being my age, going to school, having problems. I didn't ask any of the questions crowding into my mind, partly because I didn't know which one to ask first, but mostly because of the funny look on Mom's face.

An odd silence fell over us, disturbed only by Robbie's putt-putting as he motored his cars around the fireplace.

"Here's your record, Lyssie." Dad broke the weird silence. "I guess you'll be wishing you could make one of your own before long."

"It's silly wishing things like that," Aunt Reva said crossly. "More sensible to wish for supper."

Laughing, Mom went out to the kitchen.

"I'm not sure it's sensible to wish at all," I said softly.

Dad looked at me. "Surely Lyssie the wisher isn't going to give up wishing. Not with a sky full of stars still up there waiting."

"Wishing is foolishness," Aunt Reva said.

"But fun," Dad said. "That is if you don't count too much on your wishes coming true."

"You're too much of a romantic, Hewitt. It's no wonder you've never made any money."

"I've never wished for more," Dad said.

Aunt Reva's eyes jerked up to find mine. "Nobody should wish for money. Ever."

"I'm not going to wish for anything," I said quietly.

Aunt Reva relaxed a bit in her chair before she said, "What's taking Vivien so long with supper?"

"I'll go help her," I said, glad of an excuse to get away from the puzzled look growing in Dad's eyes.

I left my sweater over the mirror that night, and the next morning I combed my hair in the bathroom. Just before I left for school I started to lift the sweater off, but then I pulled my hands away. What if I couldn't keep my mind from thinking a wish? In the bathroom I'd already caught myself "wishing" Robbie would go away and stop asking so many questions. What if the mirror had caught that wish?

At school I felt like I'd been put together all wrong, as though my clothes didn't match, as if nothing I said would make any sense. On the way to school I had decided to avoid Doug altogether, but he was waiting in the hall for me when I went through the front doors.

I wanted to talk to him, but at the same time I knew I wouldn't be able to say any of the right things. I'd never been able to talk to boys. Not before I'd wished it in Millicent's mirror. Now as I watched him push away from the wall to come meet me, I wanted to run home, yank the sweater off the mirror, and wish I didn't feel so tongue-tied.

75

"Hi, Alyssa," he said. "I've been watching for you."

"Oh." I went absolutely blank. Then as I shifted my books uneasily in my arms, the record slipped and almost fell. I caught it and said, "Here's your mother's record."

"Did you listen to it?" Doug asked as he took it from me.

"Three times."

"You liked it that much?" He raised his eyebrows.

"Mom and Dad did. After they listened to it a time or two, they remembered it well enough to sing along."

We had turned and begun easing our way along the hall through the other kids to my locker.

"I guess they are about the right age to remember."

I looked at him. "How would you know?"

"I met your father and your little brother the other day. He's got a nice little store."

"Yes," I said, remembering that Marci had said her father was a bank president.

"He said you helped out there sometimes."

"Sometimes."

Doug grinned at me. "He told me about how you used to make up songs about the apples and wild stories about the lives of the people who came in to buy them."

My face turned red. I could just imagine Dad talking, telling Doug all kinds of stories about me once he found out that Doug knew me. "Dad talks too much."

Doug laughed. "I thought it was interesting."

"More like embarrassing."

"Why would it be embarrassing?" He went on

without waiting for me to answer. "I used to make up songs, too."

"You don't anymore?"

"They weren't any good." His smile disappeared. "Or so I was told."

"Neither were mine, but it was fun."

"I'll bet, with your father for an audience. I liked him."

"Everybody does," I said.

I was glad the first bell shrilled through the hall just then and gave me an excuse to rush off to my locker. It wasn't that I didn't want to talk about Dad, but being in the fruit and vegetable business didn't exactly compare to being in banking. Besides Dad had had no right to tell Doug about the silly songs I used to make up.

I grabbed the books out of the locker for my first two classes, and then as I started to shut the door, I caught sight of my face in the little mirror. I hesitated a minute, staring at myself, before I slammed the door shut and ran for my first class.

I didn't talk to Marci until lunchtime. Then the first thing she said was, "Doug says he can drive us over to your house after school if it's okay." She didn't wait for me to answer but rushed on with her plans. "He can't stay, some kind of meeting, but that's all the better. We can't really talk with Doug hanging around, and lately he seems to want to hang around with us all the time."

I blushed, and she laughed her Marci-laugh that made everybody at the table look over at us and smile. She glanced around and expansively included everybody in her smile. I had to be the only one at the table not smiling, which Marci finally noticed.

"What's wrong, Alyssa? Do you have to work at your father's store this afternoon?"

"No," I said. "I don't have to work."

"Then it's all set. I'll tell Doug in chorus or maybe you'd rather. It'd give you an excuse to talk to him."

"I've already talked to him this morning."

Marci raised her eyebrows. "I can't believe my brother has finally fallen for a girl."

"Especially me?" I pushed my plate away and looked at her.

"I didn't say that. I thing you're a great choice." She began folding the top of her milk carton in and out. "It's just that Doug's never actually had very many real girlfriends."

"I don't know that I'm a *real* girlfriend either."

"Who knows what's real anyway?" Marci said. "I doubt if I've ever had a real boyfriend."

"You could have any boyfriend you wanted," I said as we began gathering our trays to take up to the window. "I'll bet at least six of the boys right here at this table would love to fill the bill."

"How can you tell?"

"I just can, and you can, too."

She sighed. "Maybe so, but they all expect me to be a certain way. If I strayed from that path then they wouldn't like me anymore."

"I don't believe the other kids expect you to be perfect before they'll like you."

"But it's true."

"I don't care if you're not perfect."

Marci smiled and gave me a quick hug. "I know, and that's why you're like a wish come true."

After we found our seats in Algebra class, I couldn't keep my mind on the x's and y's of the equations on the board. Marci's words kept echoing in my head. A wish come true. That's what my friendship with her really was, but I felt guilty when I remembered I'd made the wish in the mirror to begin with because

78

Marci was so pretty and popular. I'd thought she was perfect, just as she'd said.

When I glanced over to where she sat across the room, she must have felt my look because she smiled and then made a silly face at the teacher, Mr. Barnes. I had to swallow my giggle as Mr. Barnes turned to fasten his eyes straight on me.

After chorus that afternoon, Mr. Birdsong reminded me about my voice lesson the next morning at ten o'clock. Then Doug drove Marci and me to Aunt Reva's house.

We were both sitting up front with Doug, me in the middle, and I'd felt sort of fluttery inside all the way from school.

As Doug pulled to a stop in front of the house, he said, "I wish I didn't have to go to that meeting. I've always wanted to see the inside of this house."

"Me, too," Marci said. "It's supposed to be haunted or something. Somebody got murdered here or something, right, Doug?"

"You never get anything right," Doug said. "No murders. Just something mysterious about a young girl's tragic death. She fell or something."

"Now I remember the stories," Marci said. "She fell out a window, and then she came back to haunt the place. But what if she didn't fall? What if she were pushed? That could be murder."

"Don't be overdramatic, Marci," Doug said.

"What was her name?" I asked, every muscle still as I waited for an answer.

"Mary. Meredith. Something like that, wasn't it, Doug?"

"I don't remember," Doug said. "What difference does it make anyway? They were all just a lot of tales."

"Yeah, the kind that makes tingles run up and down

your spine when you're a little kid," Marci said. "But what really made the place scary was old Miss Reva."

"She's still here," I said.

"I thought she was ancient when I was a kid. I can't believe she's still alive," Marci said.

"Maybe I won't go to the meeting," Doug said.

"You have to go to the student council meeting," Marci said. "You're the president."

"You can come back another time," I offered.

Doug looked over at me as Marci climbed out of the car. "How about tonight?"

I hesitated, and Marci stuck her head back in the car to say, "Say yes, Alyssa, so he'll go away."

"I guess it'd be all right, but really the house isn't haunted."

After a quick check to see if Marci had turned away, Doug touched my hand and said, "I know. That's not the reason I want to come."

"For heaven's sake, Alyssa, come on. You and Doug can hold hands later."

"Oh hush, Marci," Doug said, but he smiled at me as I climbed out after her. "See you later then, Alyssa."

Smiling back, I tried to think of something to say, but Marci was pulling me away from the car. "Brothers," she muttered under her breath. So I just waved and tried to get my heart to stop beating so hard as Marci and I went in the front door.

Mom and Aunt Reva were on the sun porch again, Mom making baskets, Aunt Reva napping. Marci was disappointed with Aunt Reva. She was just an old lady who actually almost smiled when she opened her eyes to be introduced to Marci. It wasn't really a friendly smile, but it was a smile nevertheless.

"So you're the singer's daughter," Aunt Reva said. "The one with the big house and the maid."

"I told them about going to your house last night," I said quickly and hoped Aunt Reva wouldn't say anything else.

"Oh, don't get so flustered, girl," Aunt Reva said. "That's the sole advantage to getting old. A body can say whatever they like without worrying what anybody else thinks, because nobody likes old people anyway."

"Aunt Reva, you know that's not true," Mom said. "We all like you."

Aunt Reva waved away her words. "You ask the girls there that."

"Of course Alyssa likes you, and Marci just met you. Sometimes I think you try to be rude."

"Is that a fact, Vivien?" Aunt Reva smiled again, and then the smile faded as she fastened her eyes on Marci. "I remember you. You're one of the little hooligans who used to ring my doorbell and run away."

Marci flushed crimson. It was the first time I'd seen her blush so vividly.

"I thought so," Aunt Reva said and then sank back in her chair and closed her eyes, shutting us all out.

Mom jumped in to try to ease Marci's embarrassment. "Aunt Reva sometimes likes to see if she can upset people. She really doesn't mean it."

A snort came from Aunt Reva, but she didn't open her eyes.

"It wasn't very nice of us kids," Marci admitted. Then recovering some of her poise, she began looking at the baskets hanging from the rafters. "You made all of these?" she asked, a touch of wonder in her voice. "Alyssa didn't tell me you were an artist."

Mom smiled. "There is an art to making baskets, but I'm not sure I could be called an artist. Maybe a craftsman."

Marci was walking around under the baskets, gingerly touching first one and then another. "What do you do with them all?"

"People buy them," Mom said as she calmly kept weaving a new basket. "I send them to a few gift shops around the country that sell them on consignment for me."

"I want one," Marci said.

Mom didn't hesitate. "Pick one out."

Aunt Reva raised her head. "Make her pay, Vivien. Maybe if she pays enough, you can get a maid. You'll need one when the baby comes."

"Aunt Reva," Mom said in the same firm, no nonsense voice she used to call me down when I did something wrong. Then she turned back to Marci. "Do you see one you like?"

I was relieved when Marci turned her attention to the baskets and didn't say anything about the baby even though her eyes had gotten wider when Aunt Reva mentioned it. After she'd picked out a small oval-shaped basket, she said, "But of course I want to pay you for it."

"That little basket hardly takes any time to make," Mom said. "I want you to take it as a gift."

"Are you sure?" Marci asked. Mom nodded and Marci smiled. "Then thank you. I really appreciate it. Maybe I can pay you back sometime by helping Alyssa babysit," she added with a sideways glance at me.

"It'll be awhile yet before I need a babysitter, but I'll keep you in mind." Mom laughed and touched her stomach, barely rounded under her jeans.

I practically had to pull Marci off the sun porch and upstairs. It wasn't until I opened the door of my room that I remembered the sweater draped over Millicent's mirror.

Chapter 9

I wanted to slam the door and drag Marci back to the sun porch before she could see it, but she was already in the room taking in the unmade bed, the shoes in the middle of the floor, and the sweater tied neatly over the mirror.

"I was late this morning, so it's sort of a mess," I said as I pulled the covers up on the bed and smoothed them down. I wondered what would happen if I wished the room clean. I dared a look at the mirror, but I didn't make the wish.

"I like a good mess," Marci was saying. "But I do have to admit you have a weird place to hang your sweater." Marci went over and lifted the bottom of the sweater.

"The mirror catches the light in the morning and bothers me. I guess it does look a little strange." When I moved in front of her and lifted the sweater off the glass, the mirror sparkled brighter than ever. I turned away from it without looking at my reflection.

Marci ran her hand along the frame. "It's so pretty. A fairy-tale mirror."

As I sat down on the bed and watched Marci stare at herself in the mirror, I could almost feel the mirror reaching out and grabbing her image.

"Where'd you get it?" she asked.

"Aunt Reva told me I could bring something down from the attic for my birthday. There's all kinds of junk up there."

"This isn't exactly junk."

"But it's old. It belonged to her sister, Millicent, and Aunt Reva said Millicent died years ago."

"Did you say Millicent?" Marci finally turned away from the mirror to come sit on the end of the bed. Still her eyes kept shifting back to the mirror.

When I nodded, Marci bounced around on the bed to stare at me. "That's the name," she said. "That's the name of the girl who's supposed to haunt this house. Do you know what happened to her?"

"I asked Aunt Reva, but she gets cross when I ask questions. Mom says Robbie and I get on her nerves because she's never been around kids that much."

Marci made a face. "Imagine her remembering me from when I used to ring her doorbell. I didn't think she ever even saw me."

"Do we have to talk about Aunt Reva? It's bad enough that I have to put up with her all the time downstairs."

"But aren't you curious about what happened to Millicent? I mean especially now that you know she didn't die a natural death or anything."

"No," I lied.

"But she might be haunting you. You might see her ghost."

"That's all just a bunch of stories like Doug said."

"Maybe, but Doug didn't know there was a real Millicent." Marci slipped off her shoes and tucked her feet up under her. Her eyes flashed with excitement. "Do you think if I spent the night I might see her ghost wandering through the halls?"

"There's no ghost," I said flatly as I got off the

bed. "You want to go down and find something to eat?"

"Will your Aunt Reva be in the kitchen?"

"No, she takes a nap about this time of the day."

"Let's go then. Maybe we can talk to your mother again. She's something." Marci stood up. "Is she really going to have a baby?"

"I'm afraid so."

"Don't you want her to?"

"Would you want your mother to have a baby?"

Marci laughed. "My mother? Sometimes I wonder if she hired somebody to have me and Doug. You know, like some people do nowadays. I mean can you imagine my mother with a big stomach and swollen feet? Marcella Devine? Impossible."

"Nothing's impossible."

"That is," Marci said. "But I think it's neat that your mother's going to have a baby. What do you want? A baby sister or brother?"

"I haven't thought much about it one way or the other."

"You're as cranky as old Miss Reva." Marci frowned at me. "You sound like you wish she wasn't pregnant at all."

"I haven't wished that," I said with a quick glance back at the mirror. "I'm just a little worried about her. Having a baby's harder on you after you get as old as she is, but I'd never wish she wasn't pregnant. She and Dad are too happy about the whole idea."

"Don't get in a panic," Marci said as we went out into the hall. "It wouldn't be that bad if you had thought it, especially if you're worried about her."

"But I didn't," I insisted again even though I knew it wasn't entirely true. But I couldn't think about it now. The mirror was listening.

That night after supper, Doug showed up at the

door as promised. I introduced him to everybody, and then because the night was warm, we went out to sit in the old glider on the porch. Robbie followed us, asking Doug one dumb question after another.

When Dad came out to chase Robbie back indoors, he stopped a minute to gaze up at the sky. Doug made the mistake of saying something about the stars and planets, and Dad launched off on one of his favorite theories—that all life has some kind of basic connection and that this unseen force could span galaxies to join us with all other life forms wherever they were and no matter how alien.

"But I'm boring you," Dad said finally.

"Not at all," Doug said, and I could tell he really meant it.

"Well, even if I'm not boring you, I definitely am Lyssie. She's heard it all a million times before." Dad smiled at me. "She used to throw in a few novel theories of her own."

"Dad," I pleaded. The last thing I needed was for Dad to start telling Doug some of the crazy things I used to dream up. "I was just a kid then."

Dad's smile changed until it looked almost sad. He clapped Robbie on the shoulder. "Come on, Robbie. How about you and me taking a ride out of town away from all these lights so we can find a place where we can really see the stars?"

As Robbie ran into the house to tell Mom and get some blankets for their stargazing trip, Doug said, "That sounds like great fun, Mr. Blake. Do you think Alyssa and I could come along?"

Dad hesitated and looked at me. "What about it, Lyssie? Want to go stargazing?"

"Sure. Why not?" I said, glad that my face was in the shadows.

A few minutes later we were all piled into Dad's

old truck with Robbie squirming in Doug's lap trying to twist every which way to see the sky out the window. Outside of town Dad pulled the truck off the road beside a wide, open field where no lights spoiled the black of the night.

While Robbie and Doug were clambering out the other door, Dad squeezed my knee and whispered in my ear, "Sorry about this, Lyssie. I didn't mean to mess up your date."

"It's okay. I like to look at the stars."

"But it's not exactly what you were wishing for, I'll bet."

"I wasn't wishing for anything," I said softly.

Dad patted my knee as he opened his door. "But if you see a shooting star, you have to wish on it. That's required for everybody," he said as he climbed out of the truck.

I slid out on my side, and Doug was waiting to help me down. I wondered what I would have wished in the mirror if I had allowed myself to wish. We might have gone to a movie or out to eat, but I would never have dreamed of wishing to go stargazing with my father and little brother. Still, Doug seemed happy enough about the whole situation, and I didn't have to worry about what I'd say. Robbie did enough talking for all of us.

Finally after we'd spread the blankets on a flat space in the field and lay down with our heads in a circle and our bodies making spokes of a wheel, Dad quieted Robbie by saying, "If you keep talking so much, you'll scare the stars away."

Robbie giggled but quit talking. Then silence fell over us, deep and complete as we listened to the night and let the majesty of the sky soak into our beings. I'd forgotten how special stargazing could be. As I lay there tracing the patterns of the stars and watching more and more of them materialize as my eyes adjusted to the darkness, my only worry was that Doug would think we were all crazy.

So when a meteor traced a path across the heavens, I made a wish without thinking. I didn't exactly put my wish into words but just sort of threw my feelings up toward that fiery tracer across the black sky.

A few minutes later a hand sought out mine in the darkness, and I didn't mind at all that this wish had come true.

Dad began pointing out the constellations, and when Robbie begged him to tell the story of one of them, he told us about Perseus saving Andromeda from the sea monster.

With the familiar words playing across my mind, I had no trouble spotting the star-outlined shapes of brave warriors and beautiful maidens in the heavens.

After a long time we gathered up the blankets and made our way back to the truck. Dad let Doug drive while he held Robbie, who fell asleep as soon as the truck started moving.

None of us said much. I knew Dad was shuffling words in his mind into a poem, and Doug was concentrating on driving the old truck.

At the house, Dad carried Robbie inside and left Doug and me alone on the steps.

Somehow my hand was in Doug's again.

"That was wonderful," Doug said. "I don't know when I ever enjoyed anything so much."

"You'll probably have grass chiggers in the morning," I said.

"Then I'll scratch them, but I won't regret stargazing with you."

He put his finger under my chin and lifted my face up to look at him. I was glad our faces were shadowed in the dim light filtering out through the windows since I was sure my eyes would betray the panic growing inside me at the thought of him kissing me. I wished fervently I knew how to kiss. I needed magic. Maybe more than magic.

He must have sensed my feelings, because he just traced his finger across my cheek and said, "I'll call you. Okay, Alyssa?"

"Okay." I felt even more confused than ever when disappointment surged through me. Even if I had been nervous and a little scared, I'd still wanted to be kissed.

He dropped my hand and started toward his car. "Tell your dad thanks. I'd never looked at the stars like that before."

After Doug left I looked up at the sky. The stars, blotted out by the lights of the town, were fewer here, and though I watched the sky until my neck ached, I couldn't spot a single shooting star to wish on.

I went inside, called good night to Mom and Dad in the living room, and ran upstairs where Millicent's mirror caught the overhead light when I switched it on and winked at me, begging for a wish.

I turned the light off and got ready for bed in the dark. But it was a long time before I went to sleep. I kept thinking it was no worse wishing for a kiss in Millicent's mirror than wishing to hold hands on a shooting star. They were both wishes. Why did one seem innocent and the other wrong? What was it about the mirror that scared me?

I opened my eyes and looked toward it. The mirror could capture no light tonight, and I was glad.

I wondered if Millicent had lain awake like this and looked at the mirror hidden by the darkness. What wishes had she made, and what had happened to her?

When I fell asleep, I dreamed I was trapped in a room of mirrors. Everywhere I looked I saw only myself. I kept pushing against the mirrored walls, my hands pressing against the hands in the mirrors. Then suddenly when I pushed against a mirror, my reflection disappeared, and I was toppling out a window.

I jerked awake before I hit the ground. Trembling, I stared at the darkness around me and wanted to creep into Mom and Dad's room like I used to when I was little and had a bad dream.

I remembered how Dad would pick me up and carry me back through the house to my room without turning on any lights.

"The dark is good," he'd say.

"But I'm afraid of the dark," I'd whimper.

"No, you're afraid of the bad thing that happened in your dream, not the dark. The dark has a special sound. Almost like a song. Can you hear it?"

And I would listen and begin to hear the rhythm of the dark that somehow soothed my fears and made me forget my bad dreams.

I'd made up words to go with the night's song. I hadn't thought of that song for years, but now every word came back to me and I whispered them softly into the dark air.

"The darkness has a song it plays all night long, so sweet and deep it helps me sleep. Morning will bring the sun to sing a different song all the day long."

The next thing I knew it was morning, and the mirror was catching the sunlight washing through the window and sending back sparks.

After a look at my clock, I ran for the bathroom. I had just an hour to get to the school to meet Mr. Birdsong for my first voice lesson.

Chapter 10

Mr. Birdsong hopped around just as much as he did in chorus, but there all similarity between Birdie, the sweet, muddling chorus director, and Mr. Birdsong, private voice instructor, ended. The first time I strayed off-key, he jumped up from the piano and stopped me.

"You must not settle for less than perfection, Alice."

I sang through the song again, not getting it at all perfect. He banged his hand against his ear and flew in a circle around me. "Your ears. Use your ears," he shouted. "Singing is not all mouth. Singing is ears and lungs and brain and most of all heart." He thumped his chest and then poked mine. "You must learn to use your heart most of all, Alison."

I sang the same song over and over until I was sick of it. Three times I almost broke into tears and ran out of the room and home. This wasn't what I'd expected voice lessons to be. I'd expected if not fun, then certainly not torment. If not praise, then not such forceful criticism.

But I had wanted voice lessons. I had wished for them. So I pushed back the tears of frustration and forced my voice to reach for the notes as Mr. Birdsong insisted I could.

When the hour was up, I was relieved and yet at

the same time fearful that Mr. Birdsong would cancel the lessons because I hadn't shown as much talent as he had expected me to.

He dropped his hands from the keys of the piano and sat quietly looking at me. I had never seen him that still.

"Perfection is not easy," he said with the shadow of a smile. "And for most not worth the price. Sometimes, even, perfection is not possible, only something to be wished for."

I pushed the image of the mirror out of my mind.

"Or worked for," he went on. "Do you wish to continue?"

"Today?"

"No. A voice, any voice has limitations, and yours is weak yet. No, next week."

"Yes."

"Very well. Go home and learn to breathe."

He jumped up and demonstrated, then watched closely as I inhaled and exhaled until I thought I'd hyperventilate. Finally he was satisfied. "Go. Go practice, Lisa."

So all afternoon as I sacked up apples and oranges for people in Dad's store, I practiced grabbing lungfuls of air and letting it back out. I was in the store by myself. Dad had gone home to sit with Aunt Reva so Mom could take Robbie birding.

I didn't really mind keeping the store by myself, but when there were no customers, I missed Dad's stories and his crazy theories and his laughter. I wondered if he was making Aunt Reva laugh.

Yet Dad, who could make nearly anybody smile just by smiling at them, hadn't been the one to bring the first laugh out of Aunt Reva. I'd done that. Then it had been such a strange laugh that I hadn't been sure that it was a laugh at all.

Still, surely she had once laughed, I thought as I carefully lined up a new row of Granny Smith apples in one of the display boxes. Surely when they were growing up, she and Millicent had shared secrets and giggled about silly things. I thought of the picture I'd brought down from the attic. In it they were both so serious as they stared out at the camera without the hint of a smile on either face. Millicent so pretty and Aunt Reva so plain.

Yet they were sisters near the same age. They had to have laughed together. I put the last apple in the line, then went back to sit behind the counter to wait for a customer.

When I was little, I used to wish I had a sister. I could remember shutting my eyes and filling out a picture of her in my mind. Sometimes I pretended she was my twin, but she was never exactly like me. I let her hair be longer and her eyes closer to blue than to gray. Other times I'd wish her older than me so that she could explain how it felt to be seven and in the second grade, or she'd be younger so that I could teach her things like how to read the scale when I helped Dad weigh the fruit.

I had been so excited when I found out Mom was going to have a baby, but then Mom had gotten sick. Even after Robbie was safely born, not only was he not my wished-for sister, he was much too tiny to be a playmate of any kind. All he had done for months was cry and eat.

So I had easily returned to my game of pretend with my wished-up sister.

The clock on the bank across the street flashed three thirty-six. At home Aunt Reva would be demanding to get up from her nap.

Dad had asked me to stay with Aunt Reva this afternoon, but I'd begged to stay at the store instead. I hadn't been able to face the thought of being shut up in that house all day with nobody but Aunt Reva. Aunt Reva and the mirror.

A woman came in and bought a cabbage head and a bunch of bananas, but she barely disturbed my thoughts. The bell hadn't stopped jangling from the door shutting behind her before I was wondering if it might have been better for me to have stayed with Aunt Reva. Maybe I could have gotten her to talk about Millicent.

If I knew what happened to Millicent, I thought the other things I couldn't understand might become clear. And I could start wishing again.

It felt funny to feel guilty, almost afraid to wish. It felt even stranger to think my wishes would all come true. I thought again of the sister I used to dream up, and I half-wished her true so that I could have somebody to tell about the mirror.

I thought of Marci. What would she think if I told her that she liked me because I'd wished it in a mirror? In my mind I could see her backing away from me as though I had turned green or something.

I was glad a rush of customers crowded the thought out of my mind. I was so busy that it was a few minutes before I noticed Marci standing at the back of the store.

When at last the store emptied out, Marci came up to the counter. For some reason she looked uneasy as she said, "Hi. I didn't know you were working today."

It did feel funny talking to her across the counter. "Dad's staying with Aunt Reva this afternoon."

"You're here all by yourself?"

"It's not hard. I just have to weigh and sack up the produce and take their money."

"That sounds like fun. I might work at the bank

94

next summer. Mother's against it, but Daddy says it's good to have a little work experience no matter what you plan to do later on." Marci picked an apple out of the box nearest her. "It's okay if I buy an apple, isn't it?"

"Sure. But you don't have to pay for it. You can just have it."

"No. I want to see you in action." She handed me some money with a grin, then watched closely while I weighed the apple and made change. After pocketing her change, she began shining the apple on her shirt and said, "Doug said you studied the stars last night. Sounds romantic."

"Maybe. If Robbie and Dad hadn't been along." I brushed scattered shreds of onion skin off the counter and kept my eyes away from her.

"No, Doug thought your father was great. He's done nothing but talk about him all morning, so since I was down here at the bank with Daddy, I thought I'd come over to maybe see him." She took a bite of her apple and chewed awhile before she went on. "I mean, your mother was so fantastic that I couldn't believe your dad was that great, too."

"Your mother is nice." I looked up at Marci, but she was staring down at the apple. "She's beautiful and famous."

"She was famous. That's different from being famous." Marci shrugged a little and bit into the apple again. After a minute, she said, "And Daddy's a great guy. I didn't mean he wasn't. He always gives me everything I ask for. It's just that, well, everything is so relaxed at your house, and Doug has talked and talked about your father. Of course Doug and Daddy are always fighting about something."

"Oh. What about?"

"Right now it's about Doug going to college next

year. Daddy wants Doug to study economics or whatever and go into banking, and Doug is arguing for pre-med. While I can't imagine Doug as a doctor, that's all he's ever wanted to be.''

A couple of customers came in, and Marci munched on the apple and watched me wait on them.

After I had packed their sacks, tomatoes and bananas on top, and they had left, Marci asked, ''Can I do the next one?''

I looked over at her. ''Why?''

She threw her half-eaten apple in the trash and said, ''Please let me, Alyssa. It looks like so much fun, and I promise to stay and help you till closing time. Please.''

So Marci scooted around behind the counter with me, and when the next person came in, I let her weigh the potatoes and take the money and ring it up on Dad's old cash register.

At closing time, she waited while I locked the door and then asked if she could come to my house for dinner on Sunday. ''It's Celina's day off, and Mother and Daddy are going to some kind of luncheon, and Doug is doing something or other and won't be there. Your mother won't care, will she?''

''I don't think so,'' I said. ''But mealtimes are pretty weird sometimes with Aunt Reva around.''

''I like weird things.'' Marci laughed and added, ''I like you, don't I?''

I smiled, but the smile didn't sink very deep inside me. Marci didn't notice as she grabbed me in a quick hug. ''I'm so glad we're friends, aren't you? I mean special friends.''

''Of course I am.''

''I've never had a friend I could tell everything to before. I wish you'd moved here years ago.'' She rushed off to catch her father before he left the bank.

The bank wasn't open on Saturday, but her father worked every day, Marci said, except Sunday.

As I walked home I thought about Marci and how she'd chattered on and on about Mom and Dad. She'd kept saying how much she liked me and my family, that I was "different" from other girls she'd been friends with, that my family was special because we appreciated the simple pleasures of life like stargazing.

By the time I turned the corner to go the last block to Aunt Reva's house, I was beginning to wonder if she liked me at all or if she just liked the idea of being friends with the daughter of a basket weaver and a fruit vendor who she thought was living some kind of idealized life where money and possessions weren't important.

Maybe a wished-for friendship wasn't the best kind of friendship, I thought as I saw Aunt Reva's house ahead and imagined I could see a flash of light from the mirror through my upstairs window. But then I reminded myself that I had wished for friendship with Marci because she was popular and pretty—the person I'd thought her to be.

I'd wished for a friend. I'd been given a friend, and even though I knew Marci wasn't perfect now, I wasn't sorry my wish had come true. Still, I couldn't help wondering if Marci would have wanted to be my friend if I hadn't wished it in the mirror.

And Doug? Had I only wished him into liking me? He was so cute, yet with that deep look to his eyes. I remembered how my hand had felt in his as we had watched the stars the night before, and I wanted him to have held my hand because he wanted to and not because I had wished it.

I would put the mirror away. I'd take it up to the

attic and stuff it back out of the way in a corner where it couldn't catch any light.

Yet when I was in my room, looking into the mirror, I didn't lift it away from the wall. Instead I sat down in front of it and stared at my reflection. All at once I was remembering how nervous I'd been when I'd thought Doug was going to kiss me the night before.

Almost without conscious thought, I whispered, "If Doug kisses me, I wish that I would know how to kiss him back."

I hadn't wished that Doug would kiss me, I reassured myself as I went down the stairs to help Dad with supper. Mom and Robbie still hadn't come home. And I didn't see what one little wish a day could matter. I wouldn't wish for money or anything like that. Just little things, that's all. Wishing in a mirror was no different from wishing on a star, and I hadn't felt anything wrong with that the night before. Especially not after Doug had reached over to take my hand.

As we ate our beans and hot dog supper, I kept glancing up to find Aunt Reva's eyes on me. Each time I'd shift uneasily in my chair and look away, concentrating on listening to Robbie tell about the birds he'd seen that afternoon.

Then I began to feel her eyes on me all the time, and finally I looked straight at her and wished that her staring at me didn't bother me. In my mind I sent the wish around the corners, up the stairs, and through my closed door to the mirror. And like magic, her stare didn't bother me anymore, and I smiled at her.

She muttered something and looked down at her plate.

Dad laughed, mistaking her mutter for a complaint.

"Don't you like wieners, Aunt Reva? I'm sorry, but I can't cook much else."

"I like wieners all right," she said. "But there are other things I don't like so well."

She looked at me again, but it didn't bother me. I felt set free inside as if I'd had a heavy weight lifted off me, and at the same time a sense of power swept through me.

Aunt Reva didn't look at me again until I was spooning out the last bit of the fruit salad Dad had fixed for dessert. Then almost timidly, she said, "I'm ready to go back in the living room. Alyssa can help me if she's finished."

Since nothing she could do or say was going to bother me now, I jumped up to get her walker from the corner.

She waited until we were in the living room before she stopped a minute to listen behind her. When she was satisfied that Mom and Dad and Robbie weren't paying any attention to us, she said, "Look at me, girl."

I did without any hesitation. "Is something wrong, Aunt Reva?"

"You know there is. You didn't put that wicked mirror away."

"How can a mirror be wicked?"

Her face changed as her usual scowl was replaced by a sadness so deep that every wrinkle, every line of her face stood out. "You've given in to its power."

"I don't know what you're talking about, Aunt Reva."

"I should have never let you keep the mirror, but it was all so long ago. And I thought surely I must have been mistaken about the mirror."

"You're tired, Aunt Reva. Here, let me fix your

chair." I fluffed her pillow and picked up the brightly colored afghan she liked to keep over her knees.

Aunt Reva sat down and let me drape the afghan over her. "You don't know what you're doing, girl. It'll turn on you like it did Millicent."

"Why do you care? I didn't think you even liked me."

"What do you mean? Of course I like you. You're family. The only family I've got. It's just that sometimes . . ." Aunt Reva stopped and looked away from me to fasten her eyes on a spot on the wall behind my head.

"Sometimes what?" I asked.

She sighed and without looking back at me went on. "Sometimes you remind me too much of myself. Like you, I enjoyed being pretty and the young men coming to call on me. I've always wondered if I did lord it over Millicent and somehow make her resent me, but it wasn't my fault that Father loved me best. Not my fault that I was prettiest and the young men liked me, but then maybe none of that really mattered. It was that mirror."

"What about the mirror?" I stared down at her. I'd asked the question, but at the same time I didn't want to hear whatever she was going to say.

"You know." She looked at me. "You know only too well."

"I don't have any idea what you're talking about."

Aunt Reva turned her eyes back to that same spot on the wall again as if she were looking into the past. "She used to talk to the mirror. I could hear her from my room. Not the words, just the sound. She'd stop if I went to her room."

"And did the mirror talk back to her?" I said with a smile.

Aunt Reva's eyes narrowed on me. "Oh, you can

laugh now. Millicent laughed for a while, too, but then it turned on her. It'll turn on you, too. It's wicked."

"It's not that bad, Aunt Reva."

"Tell Millicent that. Or my mother and father. Or me."

"What do you mean?" I asked, my smile finally slipping away and a bit of uneasiness awakening inside me in spite of my wish.

"There's only one thing to do," Aunt Reva muttered so low that I had to strain to hear what she said.

"What's that?"

"Go away, girl." She dropped her eyes to her hands in her lap. "I need to rest now."

I stared at Aunt Reva huddled down in her chair for a minute before I shrugged and went out to the kitchen to help Mom with the dishes.

As I ran the water into the sink and half-listened to Mom and Robbie as they brought the dishes in from the table, I told myself I didn't have any reason to feel so strange, almost guilty. I hadn't done anything wrong.

Still, the feeling clung to me until I went back upstairs to my room and looked at the mirror. Then, oddly enough, the strange uneasiness disappeared.

I sat down in front of the mirror and watched myself do Mr. Birdsong's breathing exercises.

Chapter 11

I got up singing the next morning. The day was beautiful, the sun was shining, and the mirror was sparkling. I couldn't understand now when I looked at the mirror why I had worried about it so much before.

So what if it had some kind of magic. What was wrong with a little magic in your life? I began singing an old song about magic, humming when I didn't remember the words.

Raising my window, I leaned against the screen to smell the yellow and white chrysanthemums that bloomed in the small garden below.

The screen popped out and crashed to the ground. The song died on my lips as I looked down. Until that moment I hadn't remembered, but once more in my dreams I had fallen out of a window, just as Millicent had fallen out of a window in real life.

Was this the very window she'd fallen from? Was she, like me, just leaning out to catch a breath of fresh, crisp air and leaned too far?

I stared down at the screen broken apart on the stone walk below and imagined a girl lying there. A pretty girl in a black dress. But there was something wrong with the picture, and then I remembered Aunt Reva's words from the night before. "Not my fault that I was prettiest."

My legs suddenly felt weak, and I eased back inside the window and shoved it shut. Crossing over to the mirror, I picked up the picture of Aunt Reva and Millicent from the table. Aunt Reva had said she was the pretty one.

I stared for a long time at the young girl who was facing the camera without a smile perhaps, but with a look of expectation, a look of eager trust that good things were going to come her way. Could this be the young girl Aunt Reva felt like? It was too much for me to imagine.

I shifted my eyes to the other girl, whose plainness was accented by the prettiness of her sister next to her. I tried to read her look, but age had darkened the picture and spread a brown shadow over this girl's eyes. Yet I'd been able to see the prettier girl's eyes.

Aunt Reva's eyes, for now when I looked with the sun lighting my room brightly, I could see that it was Aunt Reva. She had been pretty.

And Millicent? Millicent had been plain. Millicent had owned the mirror, and she'd given in to its power. Millicent had fallen from a window and died. Maybe in this very room.

I looked around the walls at the faded wallpaper. Then there was no place else to look but at the mirror.

I stared at it a long time before I whispered, "I wish I knew what happened to Millicent." Quickly, as if I feared an immediate answer, I jumped up and ran down the stairs.

At the table Dad and Robbie were attacking stacks of pancakes while Mom, pale around the lips, sipped a cup of tea and nibbled a piece of toast.

I grabbed an orange and sat down at the end of the table. "Where's Aunt Reva?"

"She had breakfast in her room," Mom said. "She said she needed to rest." Mom took a slow sip of her tea before she went on. "Something's bothering her. You wouldn't know what it is, would you, Alyssa?"

"How would I know?" I concentrated on stripping the peel very neatly off the orange.

"I don't know. It's just that she keeps muttering something about if the girl won't do it, then she'll have to. She's not making much sense."

"If she's not better by tomorrow, maybe we should call the doctor," Dad said. "She might have had another slight stroke."

I didn't want to talk about what was bothering Aunt Reva, so I changed the subject by saying, "You don't look like you're feeling very good yourself, Mom."

Mom's smile was a little lopsided. "Babies aren't always easy to get here, but they're worth it."

Dad reached over and covered Mom's hand with his. "I tell you what. You go take a nap or read a book. Take the day off, and me and the kids will take care of Aunt Reva and everything else."

"I just took the day off yesterday," Mom protested with a shake of her head.

"There's no law against two days off in a row." Dad began gathering up the dishes and syrup and butter. "Lyssie the wisher will wish something nice for you. Robin the tobbin will draw a picture of a bird for you, and Hewitt the coo-ik will cook something for you."

"Hot dogs again?" She groaned.

"No, of course not. I'll cook something fancy today. I'll grill hamburgers."

Mom laughed. "Then Alyssa better use her wish to hope you don't burn them up like you usually do."

"She can wish it," Dad said with a laugh. "But it's one wish that doesn't have much chance of coming true."

I stayed outside the laughter. "Maybe I should call Marci and tell her not to come."

"Let her come if she wants to," Dad said. "She can eat burned hamburgers just like the rest of us, but it might be a good idea to call her and warn her first."

As I went out through the hall to the telephone, I heard Robbie ask, "Daddy, what's a tobbin?"

I couldn't hear Dad's answer. It would be something silly, but that didn't matter. What mattered was that I wanted to be able to join in the laughter instead of feeling so set apart.

By the time Marci showed up, the smoke was rolling up from the grill. Dad laughed at the look on her face and said, "Alyssa did warn you, didn't she?"

We ate outside in the warm autumn sunshine. Dad brought out Aunt Reva's chair, and she sat with the rest of us, but she never looked at me, not once.

After we ate the slightly charred hamburgers, Marci and I went up to my room. Just like before, the mirror seemed to draw her.

"I just love this mirror." She touched its frame. "I wish I had one just like it."

I wanted to push between her and the mirror and deflect her words before they could sink in. Would the mirror grant anybody's wish? I made myself sit still on the bed as I said, "I don't think there are any more like it."

Then as she turned away from it toward me, I almost told her about the mirror. I wanted to, but I didn't know what I'd say. The mirror grants wishes? The mirror has a way of grabbing you when you look at it? Aunt Reva says the mirror's wicked, and sometimes I almost believe her? I couldn't say any of those things without sounding crazy.

My chance to tell her about the mirror somehow

slipped away as she said, "Your father is just as nice as Doug said he was. Is he always so happy?"

"Dad says there's no use frowning when you can be laughing."

"I envy you a little, Alyssa."

"Me?"

"Yeah. Everything seems so easy here. There's no pressure. You just do what you want and everybody's happy."

I could hardly believe my ears. Marci envying my lifestyle? Finally I said, "I'm not sure anything's that simple."

"I guess not, but I like it here. Doug does, too." She came over to sit on the floor in front of me. "Oh, by the way, Doug told me to tell you he'd like to come over tonight if it was okay with you."

My cheeks warmed. "I guess I'll be here."

"He said he didn't kiss you Friday, that you didn't want him to." Marci looked up at me slyly.

"He told you that?"

"Not in so many words, but sisters have ways of finding things out," she said. "I told him he was crazy. That of course you wanted him to kiss you. You did, didn't you?"

"I thought about it," I said, trying not to turn red. I hesitated a second before I asked, "Have you ever kissed a boy?"

"Sure. Lots of times. Haven't you?" She must have guessed the answer from my face because she went on. "There's nothing to it, really. You just tilt your face up a little and let the guys do the rest. Nothing to it."

"If you say so."

"Don't worry, Alyssa. If Doug kisses you tonight—and I'll be surprised if he doesn't—it'll be great."

I sneaked a look over at the mirror and felt more confident.

"What can we do?" Marci jumped up and stretched.

"Whatever you want. Play cards? Go for a walk?"

Marci glanced at the mirror. "Let's go explore the attic. See if any more treasures are up there."

"I don't know whether we should. We're not supposed to bother Aunt Reva's stuff."

"She'll never know. She couldn't get upstairs if her life depended on it, and we won't hurt anything just looking around. There might even be another mirror up there."

"There won't be another mirror like Millicent's mirror," I said while at the same time I was thinking that there might be something else. I might find a clue that would help me solve the mystery of what happened to Millicent. Maybe the mirror had given Marci the idea to make my wish come true.

In the attic, I stirred up clouds of dust as I picked my way through the boxes over to the window. I tried to push it up, but the years had frozen it shut.

"What are you doing, Alyssa?" Marci asked.

"I just thought I'd let in a little air, but it won't budge." I looked through the dirty panes of glass at the ground far below. "Do you suppose a person could fall out of this window?"

"You mean Millicent?" Marci looked nervously over her shoulder. "You think that's where she fell?"

"I don't know. I was just wondering."

"That was all a long time ago." Marci shivered. "And maybe it didn't even happen. It could be just a lot of old stories like Doug says."

"It happened. I don't know exactly what, but something happened."

"You're making me feel creepy, Alyssa. Maybe it wasn't such a good idea to come up here after all."

"We're up here now. We might as well look around."

Marci glanced behind her uneasily one more time, but then forgot all about Millicent's ghost as she began discovering one "treasure" after another. We found button shoes so small that it was hard to believe anybody had ever worn them, and we tried on hats with plumes. We thumbed through old magazines and laughed at the prices in the advertisements.

"Everything is so old," Marci said. "It's like time just stopped up here."

"I wonder," I said as I looked around. "Maybe nothing has been put up here since Millicent died."

Marci shivered. "You're giving me the creeps again."

"But it's possible. Maybe there was so much of Millicent up here." When Marci's eyes got wide, I added, "Her things, I mean, that Aunt Reva or her mother or whoever didn't have the heart to come up here anymore."

"They thought the attic was haunted."

"Maybe." I looked around, and my eyes fell on the lamp and the boxes around it. I laughed. "Then again I think we're just wanting to think up something creepy. All that stuff over there's not that old. That lamp is what Aunt Reva sent me up here to get on my birthday, but after I saw the mirror I wanted it instead."

Marci picked up the lamp. "I don't blame you." Marci set the lamp down and brushed off her hands. "Where was the mirror?"

"There by that trunk." I pointed.

Marci lifted the things out of the trunk just as I had done that first day. She, too, admired the black dress and the long coil of hair. "Were these Millicent's?" she asked.

"I thought they were when I found them, but now I think they must have been Aunt Reva's."

"But why would her stuff be with Millicent's?" Marci's eyes were wide again. "Maybe Millicent's been up here moving everything around to suit herself."

"I think we've been up here too long. You're going weird on me."

"Sorry," she said with a sheepish grin. "I'm always letting my imagination run away with me, but it's kind of fun thinking about ghosts and stuff." She folded the black dress and handed it back to me.

As I placed the dress in the empty trunk and patted it down flat, a portion of the trunk bottom gave way like magic and revealed a secret compartment.

My heart began thudding heavily as I felt the edges of a small book and knew instinctively that it had to be Millicent's diary. Without saying anything, I piled the other dresses back on top of it as fast as I could. This was something I couldn't share.

After Marci and I trooped down to the bathroom to wash off the grime of the attic, Doug showed up to get her. Smiling at me in that special way of his, he promised he'd be over again later, and my heart did a little somersault.

But even while he was there, half my mind was still up in the attic with the book in the bottom of the trunk, and as soon as he and Marci drove away, I raced back up the stairs and pulled the book out of its hiding place.

The small book had a dry, aged smell that tickled my nose as I opened it and leafed carefully back to the first page. "Millicent and I," it began. So it wasn't Millicent's diary after all, but Aunt Reva's instead. I stared at the elaborately looped handwriting and tried to imagine Aunt Reva as a young girl with pen in hand beginning a record of her life.

"June 15. Millicent and I went to a lawn party today. I wore my best white dress, and then I didn't dare eat any of the wonderful food for fear of spoiling it.

"Rodger Hathaway held my hand, and Millicent was angry with me the rest of the afternoon. She likes Rodger, but when I told her I wished Rodger had held her hand instead of mine, she got angrier than ever. She hasn't spoken a word to me since we got home."

"June 16. Millicent's still mad at me, but I'm pretending not to notice. It's not my fault that Rodger thinks I'm pretty."

"June 17. I worked on my 'Home Sweet Home' sampler. Maybe if I give it to Millicent when I finish, she'll like me again."

And on it went. Every day a faithful account of some activity and a mention of Millicent. Sometimes there were only a few words. Other times an entire page would be filled up. Reading here and there, I turned the pages slowly.

"June 27. Rodger held my hand again today. He may try to kiss me if he can get me alone in the garden. I've been trying to imagine his lips on mine, but every time I think about it, I can't keep from laughing. Actually I'd rather James Wilkinson kissed me. I told Millicent that, but she put her hands over her ears and told me to go away. She must be in love with Rodger."

"July 1. Millicent says she'll never have a boyfriend with me around. She says I should be ashamed of the way I made eyes at Rodger when we passed him on the street, but I only smiled at him. I can't not smile."

"July 2. Millicent saw Rodger kissing me in the garden. I didn't want him to kiss me, but he did anyway. Millicent doesn't believe me."

I scanned the next few pages, but then my eyes froze on one of the entries a few weeks later. "July 27. Father took us to an auction today. He bought me a mirror, but Millicent wanted it so badly I gave it to her. I thought maybe it would make her like me again, but I'm not sure anything's going to do that. She's so sure that I'm stealing all her chances for a suitor. I can't help it if the young men who come to call like to sit with me on the porch. They might like to sit with her, too, if she would try smiling more."

As the light in the attic began to fade, I moved closer to the window. I began to skim the pages quickly, my eyes skidding to a stop every time I saw Millicent's name or a mention of the mirror.

"October 12. Millicent's talking to her mirror. I can hear her sometimes after I go to bed. I'm glad I didn't keep it. Whenever I'm in Millicent's room, it makes me feel peculiar, almost like it's watching me. Sometimes I feel like it's watching me when I'm not in her room. But maybe it's just Millicent watching me."

"October 20. We've just come home from Rodger Hathaway's funeral. He isn't the first the fever has taken, but the first among our friends. I've cried so much that I ache all over. Millicent, who liked Rodger much more than I did, has not cried at all, but even as I write this I hear her talking to that wretched mirror. The sound gives me chills."

Far below I could hear Dad calling me. I stuffed the diary back in its hiding place and scrambled down the attic stairs as quietly as I could. I waited till I was at the bottom before I called back, "Coming."

Doug was there to see me or maybe to see Dad. I

wasn't sure which, but I was just as glad that he wanted to talk to Dad while we ate our grilled cheese sandwiches and tomato soup for supper. I couldn't concentrate on what anybody was saying.

And tonight, instead of Aunt Reva staring at me, I kept looking at her as she slowly and carefully guided her spoon to her mouth. I was trying to see the young girl she'd once been, the girl who had written in the diary.

Finally she dropped her spoon with a clatter and looked up at me. "Stop staring at me, Millicent."

"Millicent?" I said softly. "I'm not Millicent."

"Then stop acting like her," Aunt Reva said crossly. Her eyes fell back to her plate, but she didn't pick up her spoon again.

"Who's Millicent?" Robbie asked.

"Aunt Reva's sister," Mom said quietly, her eyes steady on me. I knew if Doug hadn't been there she'd have insisted on knowing what was going on between Aunt Reva and me. But Doug was there, and Dad saved the uncomfortable moment by getting his guitar and suggesting a songfest.

Everybody except Aunt Reva sang a snatch of their favorite song to start off. Doug was shy at first, but before long he was singing right along and taking more turns than the rest of us.

Once while Doug and I were singing a duet, I almost forgot about the mirror and the diary and what had happened to Millicent. But then it was two minutes till nine, and Aunt Reva was demanding to go to bed.

Dad put his guitar aside and blew on his fingertips. "I guess it was time to quit. I've about worn the ends off my fingers."

Robbie's eyes got big. "Really? Let me see."

Everybody laughed, and Doug said, "I'd better go

home, too. I've got homework I've been putting off all weekend.''

I followed him out on the porch, thankful that Dad collared Robbie before he could tag along.

''That was great,'' Doug said as we walked down off the porch to the same spot where we'd said goodnight after the stargazing. ''I just don't know what you'll do next time to top that.''

''Maybe nothing,'' I said. ''Maybe you'll just have to sit with me on the swing and talk.''

''That might not be so bad.'' Doug reached over to take my hand.

My face was burning, but I tilted it up toward Doug's anyway, just like Marci had said I should. He gently covered my lips with his, and without a doubt I forgot all about the diary hidden up in the attic.

Then he was squeezing my hand and telling me he'd see me tomorrow, and the kiss was over though the warm feeling lingered inside me until I got back to my room.

There, with the mirror calmly grabbing my reflection, my curiosity about Millicent returned stronger than ever, overpowering even the memory of the kiss. The diary held the secret. I was sure of it.

I got ready for bed like always except for the flashlight clutched in my hand under the covers. When the night sounds let me know everybody was asleep, I crept out of bed and back up the stairs to the attic.

I had to know what had happened to Millicent. And if it was the mirror's fault.

Chapter 12

Just enough moonlight filtered through the attic window to give the boxes and old pieces of furniture eerie shadows, and for a moment I imagined Millicent there among the shadows watching me. My feet froze on the stairs. But I had to know. I forced myself to move through the shadow ghosts to the trunk and pull out the diary.

Once I opened it, everything except the words on the pages faded away. When the next date skipped to November ninth, I held the flashlight close to the middle of the book, but no pages were missing.

"November 9. I've been sick. I'm still so weak that I can hardly write a dozen words before I have to rest. My fever rose so high that they thought I would die, and now my hair is falling out. Mother is going to cut it all off tonight. My lovely hair. It'll take years to get it as long again."

"November 10. Something is wrong. They won't let Millicent see me. She couldn't possibly be jealous of me now. They let me look in a mirror yesterday after Mother cut off my hair. I hardly recognized myself.

"And it can't be because they're afraid she'll catch it, too, for she was in here while my fever was high. At least I think she was, but then it might have been a dream. I remember her standing over me begging me to live, saying over and over that somehow she'd undo what she'd done.''

"November 11. Millicent hasn't talked to her mirror once since my fever broke. I keep asking Mother if Millicent is sick, too, but Mother will only say Millicent doesn't have the fever. Still the look in Mother's eyes worries me. Something is wrong. I wish I could go see for myself, but when I stand up the world goes black.''

"November 12. Millicent fell out of her window and broke her back. She can't move her legs and the pain in her neck and arms is almost more than she can bear. They didn't tell me. I pushed a chair in front of me and went to Millicent's room. She cried when she saw me, and I cried when I saw her. When I found out she had fallen out of her window, I asked how she could possibly have done that. She turned her eyes away from me toward that wretched mirror and whispered that it wasn't hard if one leaned out far enough.''

"November 13. Friday the thirteenth. I wish I could have slept through this unlucky day. I went to Millicent's room again. She was half out of her head talking about unwishing or not being able to unwish. The more she talked the crazier she sounded. I begged her to calm down and start at the beginning. She grew very quiet as if searching inside herself for that beginning. Finally she looked at me and said, 'I wished you dead.'

"For a minute I didn't know what to say, but she looked so pale and shrunken there in her bed that I didn't have the heart to be angry. So I only said, 'You didn't mean it, Millie. I know that.'

"Tears came to her eyes and she said, 'May God forgive me, but I did. I was angry with you because Rodger loved you and not me and now he'll never love me. Then you got sick, and I knew I didn't really want you to die. I tried to unwish it, but it wouldn't let me. It laughed at me. I had to undo it another way.'

"I tried to reassure her by saying all sorts of sensible things, but she hardly listened. She kept begging me to bring her the mirror. I offered her a hand mirror, but she knocked it away and kept begging until I gave in.

"As weak as I am, it was all I could do to lift it off the wall and carry it over to her. 'I don't like this mirror,' I told Millicent. 'I think I should throw it out the window.'

"She almost fell out of the bed reaching for it. 'You mustn't, Reva. Promise me that you'll never break it. That no matter what happens you'll never break the mirror.'

"To calm her, I promised and propped the mirror where she could turn her head and look into it. And now I can hear her talking to it again. If I had the strength I'd go back to her room and smash the wretched thing in spite of what I promised, but my strength has drained away. Even now as I write these words, I'm trembling inside."

The writing was wobbly, and the mark of the pen trailed off the edge of the page. The next page was blank. Frantically I shuffled through the rest of the diary until at last I found a page covered with writing. She must have simply picked up the book, let it fall open wherever it would, and begun to write. I held my flashlight closer because its light was growing dim.

"November 17. I had a relapse. I had a relapse and Millicent died. Somehow the mirror did it. Or maybe I did it because I carried the wicked thing over to her. I begged them to bury it with her, but Mother said I was still out of my head from the fever. She finally promised to put it away somewhere where I would never have to see it again. She's packing a trunk with Millicent's clothes to take to the attic. I have put the dress I wore to Millicent's funeral and my long twist of hair in the trunk under Millicent's dresses, and tonight I'm going to put this diary in the secret bottom compartment. Like the mirror, I will never want to see it again. Oh, Millicent, my sister, my friend, why did you want to leave us?''

Very gently I shut the book and placed it back into its hiding place in the trunk. The flashlight cast only a faint circle of light in front of me as I walked to the stairs. The moonlight's shadows seemed to begin to sway and chant, ''Wicked. Wicked. Wicked.''

''I haven't been wicked,'' I said aloud, my voice jarring in the hush of the night. I had made no wicked wishes, nothing I needed to unwish.

Still the shadows continued to dance, and the chant seemed to grow louder. ''Wicked. Wicked.''

I almost fell down the steps in my haste to get away from them.

I'd carry the mirror back to the attic where it belonged, where it had been since Millicent died, sitting there in the dark waiting for someone to find it. It was time for it to begin waiting again.

I would have done it then, right away, but once I was in my room I knew I couldn't go back up there among the shadows tonight. Morning would be soon enough.

I slept fitfully, dreaming the dream about the room of mirrors and falling out of the window over and over. I was glad when at last I awoke to daylight.

As I combed my hair in front of it, I decided I didn't have enough time to carry the mirror up to the attic before school. I'd do it first thing when I got home.

The mirror sparkled as it caught the morning sun streaming through the window. I grabbed my books off the table below it and ran before I could imagine it was laughing at me.

At school Doug was waiting for me in the hall. When I saw him, I couldn't keep from wondering if he'd still like me after I took the mirror back to the attic or if the time he'd held my hand and kissed me would seem like nothing more than a dream.

"Do you think it's wrong to wish somebody liked you?" I asked him.

"Did you do that?" Doug smiled down at me.

"Dad calls me Lyssie the wisher."

"Nothing wrong with wishing, especially when your wishes come true."

"I'm not so sure about that." We stopped in front of my locker, but I just stared at it without opening it. After a moment, Doug worked the combination for me and swung open the door. When I caught sight of my face in the little mirror, I wanted to shut my eyes. I pulled out my books and pushed the door shut quickly.

No longer smiling, Doug put his finger under my chin and tipped my face. "If I'm a wish, I'm glad I came true."

All the kids around us faded away, and it was just the two of us. I wanted to tell Doug about the mirror and ask him to help me take it back to the attic, because I was beginning to think the mirror had some kind of weird power over me. I might need help.

"Doug," I began just as the bell rang. The noise and the rush of the corridor came back, and I couldn't say any more.

"What's the matter, Alyssa?"

"Nothing. I'd better run. I'll be late for class."

All day the thought of the mirror followed me around. It was there at lunch while Marci chattered on about the things we'd found in the attic and the likelihood of Millicent's ghost haunting us for bothering her things.

As she talked, I wondered how it would be to sit at lunch alone without Marci and the easy popularity that radiated out from her and enclosed me in her charmed circle.

Then in chorus we sang through a dozen new songs. The whole hour seemed more of a waste than ever now that I knew Mr. Birdsong could be a good music teacher if he wanted to be. Would he want to keep giving me lessons, or would that wish, too, disappear with the mirror?

After chorus, I missed my bus on purpose. I wanted an excuse to walk to Dad's fruit stand even though he hadn't asked me to come help him.

I didn't notice the closed sign in the window until I had already pushed on the locked door. I stood back and stared at the door while my heart began to thud heavily in my chest. Something was wrong.

As I walked the mile from the store to Aunt Reva's house as fast as I could, I tried to think of sane, sensible reasons Dad might have closed the stand.

He had talked about taking Aunt Reva to the doctor, or maybe Robbie had something going on at school that I had forgotten about. Dad sometimes closed up to go to school programs. Robbie might even have hurt himself on the playground at school. While I didn't want that to be true, that was better than some of the other things that kept coming to mind. At least I knew I hadn't wished that.

Nobody was home when I got there. Nobody. The

house opened its door and swallowed me into its silence. The kitchen showed no signs of lunch or after-school snacks for Robbie. Out on the sun porch, the basket Mom was working on lay as she'd left it Friday afternoon. I checked Aunt Reva's room. The spread on her bed was pulled up neatly.

At the bottom of the stairs I found Aunt Reva's walker lying on its side. Without thinking, I set it upright before I ran up the stairs, but the upstairs was as empty as the downstairs. I was totally alone.

The mirror was waiting for me. Its glass seemed to be sparkling brighter than I'd ever seen it. "Where are they?" I demanded, staring into its depths, trying to see the unseeable.

In the mirror I saw myself, pale, wide-eyed with panic, holding my hands over my ears against the silence. It was the way I'd looked in the dreams as I'd frantically searched to find my way out of the mirrors. Confused, frightened, and helpless.

When I tried to jerk the mirror off the wall, it caught and held. I almost turned it loose and let it stay, but then I took a firmer grip and pulled until the mirror came away from the wall.

With the face of the mirror turned away from me, I carried it into the hall and had just started up the attic steps when Dad came in the front door downstairs and called, "Lyssie?"

Without waiting for an answer, he bounded up the steps two at a time as if he, too, feared to listen to the silence of the house.

I didn't have time to get rid of the mirror. Dad was already behind me, saying, "There you are, Lyssie."

When I turned, the mirror caught light from somewhere and flashed.

"What are you doing with that?" Dad asked. Strain tightened every line of his face.

"What's wrong?" I asked instead of answering him. "Where is everybody?"

He forgot about the mirror. "Aunt Reva had a stroke. I don't know what got into her. She knew she shouldn't try to climb the stairs."

The mirror seemed to grow heavier until I thought I wouldn't be able to hold it. "She tried to come upstairs?"

"She was almost to the top when your mother saw her." Dad's face became sadder and grimmer. "I don't know what she was trying to do."

"She wanted to break the mirror," I said softly.

Dad looked at me as if he thought everyone in the whole world had gone crazy but him. "What are you talking about, Alyssa?"

Then when I started trying to explain about Millicent's mirror, he cut me off. "You'll have to tell me about it in the truck. We've got to get back to the hospital."

I sat the mirror down, face against the wall by the bottom of the attic stairs. "Is Mom with Aunt Reva now?" I asked as I stood back up.

"No." The lines of worry deepened on his face. "She tried to help Aunt Reva. She had to, you know, with Aunt Reva falling like that."

A dark new fear opened up in front of me, and I tumbled headlong into it. "Where's Mom?"

Dad turned his eyes away from mine. "She's in the hospital, too. She almost lost the baby."

"I didn't wish that." I yanked the mirror around and yelled at it. "I didn't wish that." The mirror didn't flash any light. It just let me look at myself. I couldn't stand it.

I grabbed it and started for the staircase. I'd throw it down the stairs. That would be sure to break it.

Dad caught my arm as I passed him. When I

whirled around, the mirror flashed a circle of silver white on Dad's face.

"What's the matter with you, Alyssa?" He shook me a little, and the light danced across his face.

"I've got to break it. Don't you see? It's all my fault. I've got to break it."

Dad took hold of the mirror, and after a minute my hands turned it loose. He gently lifted it away from me and sat it against the wall, face out. I tried to keep from looking at it.

With his arm around my shoulders, he steered me to the top of the staircase. We sat where earlier Aunt Reva had fallen. "It's not your fault, Lyssie. You didn't make Aunt Reva climb the stairs."

"I should have broken it or at least put it away when she told me to. She kept warning me that it was wicked, but I didn't want to believe it."

"What was wicked?" Dad asked.

"The mirror." I couldn't see it behind me, but I knew it was still watching me. "Millicent's mirror. It makes wishes come true."

Dad actually laughed as he hugged me closer to him. "Lyssie, my wisher. So you finally found something to make your wishes come true."

"I don't know how you can laugh."

"I don't either," Dad said. "But what else do you expect me to do when you tell me you've found a magical mirror straight out of the fairy-tale books to make your wishes come true?"

"It's not funny."

"Nor is it true, sweetheart. Mirrors don't grant wishes, but even if it were true, Aunt Reva wouldn't risk her life to destroy it. Nothing's wrong with a few wishes coming true."

"She did it for us. She did it so nothing would

happen to us like what happened to Millicent and her."

"Millicent?"

"Millicent wished Aunt Reva dead and then when Aunt Reva was dying she tried to unwish it, but the mirror wouldn't let her."

"Slow down, Lyssie. You're not making much sense, and we've got to get back to the hospital. I told your mother I'd only be gone a few minutes. Just long enough to drop Robbie off at Joey's house and get you." He stood up, pulling me up with him. "We'll have to straighten it all out later."

I glanced at the mirror. It had a way of catching light no matter where it was, and now it winked at me as if we were co-conspirators. I pulled at Dad's arm. "Break it, Daddy. Please."

He looked at the mirror and then back at me while every trace of smile drained from his face until he looked as if he'd never smiled in his life. "No."

"But Mama still might lose the baby."

"I can't believe you wished that, Alyssa."

"I didn't exactly wish it, but I wasn't glad about the baby."

"And you think the mirror read your mind and caused all this to happen?"

"I don't know. I just know it's my fault."

"No, Lyssie. It's not your fault." Dad hugged me before he started down the steps.

I dragged my feet, reluctantly following him. "Please break it," I whispered.

But Dad, already at the front door, didn't hear me.

We didn't talk in the truck on the way to the hospital. Dad's mind was completely on Mom and the baby, and though all kinds of words raced through my mind, none of them were the right ones to make

123

Dad understand about the mirror. I just knew that once more the mirror had won and that back in the hall at the house it was catching the light and laughing.

Chapter 13

At the hospital, we went to see Mom first. Her face was as white as the sheets pulled up around her. She tried to smile at us, but all the while her hands kept moving down to her small rounded belly as though she could hold the baby there.

"The doctor says I may have to stay here for a week," she said.

"As long as it takes, Vi." Dad gently pushed her hair back from her face. "You know that."

"But what about you and Robbie and Alyssa?"

"We'll manage," Dad said.

"Sure, Mom," I said from the other end of the bed. "Don't worry about us." I smiled, but I couldn't meet her eyes. I wanted to throw myself on the bed and beg her forgiveness.

But she didn't know she had anything to forgive me for, so I just kept smiling in her direction trying to look cheerful and hopeful while I sucked in lungfuls of air until I felt dizzy. After a few minutes, I slipped out of the room on wobbly legs and leaned against the corridor wall.

A nurse looked at me oddly, then hurried on down the hall. I was glad she hadn't stopped. I didn't want to talk to anybody. I just wanted to hide somewhere until it all went away. I wanted Mom to be home weaving her baskets while Aunt Reva sat in the sun.

I closed my eyes, hoping it was just a bad dream, even wishing it, but when I opened my eyes again the nurses were still talking at the nurses' station and the sound of a baby crying drifted down the hall from somewhere. No sounds came from the room behind me, and I was tempted to stick my head back through the door to see if Mom and Dad were still there.

The nurse had already hurried past me three more times on softly squishing shoes before Dad came out to find me.

"There you are," he said. "We didn't know where you'd got to."

"I thought maybe you and Mom wanted to be alone." I stared down at a dark spot on the blue carpet.

He looked back toward the door. "Your mother's sleeping now. I thought we should go and check on Aunt Reva."

We had to wait ten minutes before they let us in the intensive care unit to see Aunt Reva.

The machines hooked to Aunt Reva were beeping and pulsing and flashing, but I still had to stare hard at her chest before I was sure she was breathing.

"Aunt Reva," Dad said. "Can you hear me? Alyssa and I have come to see how you're doing."

Very slowly she opened her eyes and without even a sideways glance at Dad fastened her stare on me. Dad kept talking, telling her that she should rest and that she'd be better and out of the hospital in no time.

All the time Dad talked she kept her eyes on me. Twice she moved her lips, but no sound came out.

"Can't she talk?" I whispered to Dad.

"Not right now." Dad touched Aunt Reva's hand. "But she'll feel better soon, and then she'll be able to talk again."

"I know what she wants to say."

Dad shook his head at me before I could say any more. "We don't want to tire you out, Aunt Reva. We'll come back again in a little bit."

Even after I turned away from the bed, I could still feel her eyes on me. I let Dad get a few steps ahead of me, then looked around and met her stare squarely while I nodded my head once. She sank deeper into the bed and shut her eyes.

Back down in Mom's room, Dad watched Mom sleep while I stared out the window at the parking lot and wondered if I could really destroy the mirror as I'd promised Aunt Reva I would in the nod.

When I looked at Dad, I caught his eyes on me instead of Mom. "Maybe I should go on home," I said. "You know, get Robbie and fix our supper."

"And break the mirror?" Dad asked. "That's what you thought Aunt Reva was trying to say, wasn't it?"

"Yes," I answered.

"And are you going to break it, Alyssa?"

"If I can."

"Of course you can break the mirror, Alyssa. Breaking things is easy. Just take a hammer and smash it." Dad kept his voice low so he wouldn't wake Mom, but the look on his face was so intense that it was almost as if he were yelling at me.

"I guess that might be the best way." I looked down at the floor, imagining the mirror shattering under the blow of a hammer. I felt sick.

He didn't say anything more for so long that I was sure he had turned his attention back to Mom, but when I looked up, he was still watching me.

"I've never given you much, Lyssie." His smile was so sad that I wanted to jump up and hug him, to do something to bring back his real smile.

But I sat still, knowing he wouldn't welcome my

hug. "You've always given us everything we needed,"
I said.

"Not really. Nothing but dreams." His eyes drifted
over to my mother. "Vivien deserved better. She had
to give up so much to marry me. Her family had
money, you know, but her father disowned her when
she married me. Vivien always thought it was the
money that spoiled the love in her family. That's why
she made me promise not to get rich."

Dad laughed a little, but it wasn't a happy laugh.
"That wasn't a hard promise to keep," he went on.
"Me with my fruit and philosophy and poems."

"Some things are more important than money."

Dad didn't act like he heard me. "But it wouldn't
have mattered if we had made money. That wouldn't
have changed the way we felt about each other. And
it wasn't the money that spoiled the love between her
and her father."

"What did then?"

"I don't know for sure. Neglect perhaps. He never
had time for her." Dad was quiet for a minute. "But
maybe he did love her in his way. He just didn't know
how to show it. I suppose he thought the money was
enough to hold her to him and make her need him.
He never really thought she'd give all that up."

"He didn't know Mom very well, did he?" I said,
looking over to where Mom slept.

"Can any father ever know his daughter?"

My insides went soft as I looked back at Dad and
said, "I'll always need you, Daddy."

Dad smiled, but he still looked sad somehow. "I
didn't tell you this to make you feel bad about growing older and wanting to try out your own wings.
That's good. I told you so you could understand about
the mirror."

"What about the mirror?" I felt cold inside as I waited for his answer.

"Oh, Lyssie, my little wisher, you've always wanted to believe in magic, haven't you? And I guess that's my fault."

"I don't want to be a wisher anymore."

Dad's eyes bored into me. "It's hard to know what to wish sometimes, especially if you think your wishes are going to come true."

"They did come true. Everything I wished."

"Everything?"

"Everything. Even the things I didn't want to come true." I let my eyes touch Mom again.

"The mirror didn't make this happen, Lyssie."

"But—" I started and stopped.

"I know. But you had bad thoughts. You didn't want us to have another baby. You thought we were too old and we didn't have enough money already and another baby would just make things worse like it did before Robbie was born. I know that was a hard time for you."

I stared down at my hands.

Without any hint of disapproval, he kept talking. "They were natural enough feelings. Things your mother and I have thought about ourselves. With time you'd have thought it all through for yourself, and then the bad thoughts would have gone away."

"But the mirror captured them first," I whispered.

"The mirror didn't cause this to happen. At least not because it was magical or anything."

"What about Millicent? What about what the mirror did to her and Aunt Reva?"

"What did the mirror do to them?"

I told him about Millicent wishing Aunt Reva dead and about how she'd regretted it after Aunt Reva got sick and how she'd tried to unwish it and when she

129

couldn't, attempted to kill herself to destroy the wish. While I tried to tell it all plainly and simply, the more I talked the harder it was to make clear. It had all been so easy to understand while I was reading the diary, but now it sounded strange even to my ears.

Without comment, Dad waited till I was finished. Then he thought a minute before he said, "That wasn't the mirror. That was jealousy. Plain and simple."

"Jealousy doesn't make people sick."

"No, germs do. It was only chance that made Aunt Reva get sick at the same time Millicent was angry at her."

"And what caused my wishes to come true?" I asked, my voice so loud that Mom stirred in the bed.

"What wishes, Alyssa?" Dad said as soon as Mom settled back to sleep.

I kept my voice low. "I wished that I was prettier and then I was. I wished Marci would be my friend, and she started sitting with me at lunchtime. I wished Doug would like me." I stopped.

"And he did," Dad finished for me.

I nodded miserably.

"That's nothing to be so sad about. Doug's a nice boy." Dad waited till I looked up. "Was there more?"

"Mostly little things. Aunt Reva laughing, things like that. I guess I was sort of testing out the mirror."

"And the mirror passed the tests?"

"Everything I wished came true."

"Surely not everything," Dad said with a smile. "Or the world would be pretty messed up by now what with everybody drinking red juice for breakfast."

When I didn't smile, Dad's own smile faded. It didn't disappear. It just sank deeper until everything

130

about his face looked gentle and loving. I couldn't stand it. I looked away from him, back out the window to where the sun glinted up at me off the cars, and tears rolled down my cheeks.

After a minute, he reached over and with one hand on my cheek turned my face back to his. "All that would have happened without the mirror. Do you believe that, Alyssa?"

"I don't know," I whispered. "I want to, but Aunt Reva doesn't believe it."

"I know. For her sake, I suppose you'll have to do something with the mirror. She's too old and sick to be reasonable about it now. People always feel a little guilty when someone they love dies, especially a young person, and I suppose Aunt Reva had to find a reason for it all. Blaming the mirror must have been her way of reconciling herself to Millicent's death. Do you understand what I'm trying to say?"

"Sort of," I said, getting up. I looked at Mom and then back at Dad. "Stay as long as you want to. I'll take care of Robbie."

"I know you will." He waited till I was at the door before he added, "Don't break it, Lyssie. You don't need to break it."

As I walked away from the hospital toward Aunt Reva's house, I thought about what Dad had said. I wanted to believe it. I didn't want the mirror to have any kind of power. I wanted to believe that Marci was my friend because she wanted to be and that Mr. Birdsong had offered me voice lessons because I had talent. Most of all I wanted to believe Doug liked me simply because I was me and not because of the mirror.

But how could I get rid of it without breaking it? I could put it back where I found it, but I'd know it was there. Everytime something went wrong or I wanted something badly enough, I'd be tempted to creep up the stairs and give myself over to its power. Even if I could keep myself away from the attic, I might send it thoughts and wishes.

Just then Doug pulled up beside me and touched his horn lightly. "Need a lift?" he asked.

"Sure, thanks," I said, but even as I was climbing into the car, I was searching my thoughts to see if I'd wished him there.

"I went by your father's store," he was saying. "When I saw it all closed up I went over to your house, but nobody was home. A guy up the street told me he'd seen an ambulance there. Was it your Aunt Reva?"

I explained about Aunt Reva's stroke and how my mother had almost lost the baby. As I talked I kept thinking about Aunt Reva pulling herself up those steps one at a time to get to the mirror.

"That's awful." Doug put his hand over my hand on the seat between us.

It felt warm and good, and I wanted to just sit there and enjoy the comfort he was offering me. But when he put his hand back on the wheel to make a turn, I tucked my own hand in my lap. After I got rid of the mirror, he might not want to hold my hand anymore.

When we got to the house, Robbie was sitting on the steps all by himself.

"What are you doing here?" I asked. "You're supposed to be at Joey's."

Robbie looked up at me with big eyes. "I saw a gray bird with white spots on its wings, and I wanted to tell Mama about it."

"Mama's not here."

"I know. Daddy said she was sick." He jumped up off the step, and grabbing me around the waist, he buried his face in my shirt. "Is she going to be all right, Lyssie?"

"Of course she is," I said.

I guess I didn't sound sure enough, because Robbie went on. "Do you think if we closed our eyes and wished hard enough it could make her well?"

"No," I said sharply. Robbie stiffened at the sound of my voice, and Doug frowned at me. I swallowed and tried again in a gentler voice. "No, Robbie. We don't have to wish Mama better. She's already better. She just needs to rest a while before she can come home from the hospital."

"But it couldn't hurt to wish." Robbie looked up at me and screwed his eyes shut tight.

I made myself say, "No, it couldn't hurt to wish." I shut my mind against the thought of the mirror waiting for me up in the hall. I couldn't do anything about it with Doug and Robbie there. They'd ask too many questions I couldn't answer.

When Robbie opened his eyes, I pulled his arms away from my waist. "I've got to go call Joey's mother so she'll know you're okay, and then I'll fix us something to eat."

"How about if I go get some hamburgers?" Doug offered. "Or maybe a pizza."

Robbie began jumping up and down. "A pizza. Please, can we have the pizza?"

Doug wanted me to go with him and Robbie to get the pizza, but I told him I needed to stay at the house in case Dad called. It was partly true.

After they left and I had called Joey's mother, I went up the stairs. I lifted each foot slowly up to the next step, moving as heavily as Aunt Reva must have earlier that day. The mirror was waiting, and even though I didn't turn the hall light on, it caught light from somewhere and flashed it at me.

I didn't care what Dad said. I had to break it.

The gold frame felt warm when I picked it up. No light flashed from the mirror now. Instead it seemed to be pulling in all the light and letting none loose. My reflection was there on the glass, but I paid no attention to it as I probed the depths of the mirror.

I was in my room, holding it back up to the wall before I realized what I was doing.

I yanked it away from the wall and ran down the stairs, almost tripping halfway down and hoping that I would. Surely if I dropped the mirror here, it would break.

But the frame stuck to my hands, and even in the kitchen I had a hard time turning it loose to get the hammer. Then without looking too close at the mirror, I raised the hammer to let it fall on the glass.

"You don't have to break it." Dad's words whispered through my mind, but Dad didn't understand about the mirror. He thought it was all in my head. That the mirror had no power, no magic. The hammer was growing heavy in my hand. Breaking the mirror was the only way.

As I started to let the hammer fall, I caught sight of my white face in the mirror. My arm froze as I stared into wild eyes that couldn't be mine but were. After a second I laid the hammer on the table and sat down to study the mirror. And myself in the mirror.

Dad was right to tell me not to break the mirror. Breaking it would mean I'd given in to its power, for no matter what Dad said, the mirror did have some kind of power, if only the power my mind was giving it, believing that it was magical.

I'd put it out with the trash. Just like any other worthless piece of junk.

As I stood up, the mirror flashed light in a dozen different directions at once, but I paid it no attention.

The garbage truck would come the next day, and it was my chore every week to sack up the trash and carry it out to the curb. After I carried the trash bags out to the street, I went back for the mirror. I sat it facedown against the garbage bags. It had captured its last light and granted its last wish.

Doug and Robbie came in with the pizza as I was putting the hammer back in the drawer. It was a good pizza and tasted even better when Dad came in before we were finished eating to report that both Mom and Aunt Reva were better.

Later when Doug left, I walked out to his car with him. He held my hand and kissed me goodbye just like he had the night before when the mirror still hung on my wall.

"Why do you like me?" I asked abruptly after he kissed me.

He stumbled around looking for the right answer. "You're nice," he said. "You're different from other girls I've gone out with. I don't know. Do I have to have a reason?"

"But what made you first notice me?"

"That's easy," he said. "Your smile. And then that day you sang your solo, you looked so special while you were singing as if the song were part of you instead of just words and notes on a sheet of paper. I knew I wanted to know you better."

"I did wish you would like me," I said softly.

"I know." He squeezed my hand. "And I wished you would like me. That night we watched the stars with your father and Robbie, I wished it on a falling star."

"Then it wasn't only my wish."

He pulled me closer to him and kissed me again. "It's better when both people are wishing."

After he left, I didn't even glance over at the pile of trash as I went back inside.

The next morning as I got ready for school, my eyes kept coming back to the spot where the mirror had hung. The sun was up, and I missed the light sparkling off the mirror.

Going to the window, I pushed it up and leaned out to make sure the mirror was still where I'd left it. Light flashed back to answer yes. Someone had turned the mirror around where it could catch the sunlight, and it almost seemed to be exploding with light.

I had to turn it back around before someone saw it. I was turning away from the window when a car stopped, and a woman got out and picked up the mirror. The reflected light danced on her face as she gazed down at it.

I raced out of my room and down the steps, but by the time I got out the front door she had already put the mirror in her car and was pulling away from the curb.

Dad had followed me out of the house. "What's going on?" he asked.

"That woman took the mirror." I pointed toward her car.

"Does it matter?"

I watched the car disappear around the corner, and after a minute I said, "No."

And as the days passed, I knew it was true. It didn't matter. Even without the mirror, Marci still wanted to be friends, and Doug and I began practicing a duet with Mr. Birdsong's help. Doug says he likes singing with me, and he even wrote a song for me. We sing it when we're alone.

Mom came home from the hospital, still pregnant to my relief, and though I couldn't completely forget all my worries about the baby, I did begin to look forward to having a new brother or sister, just like Dad had said I would.

Aunt Reva had to stay in the hospital several weeks, but after she was out of intensive care, Dad made sure we went to see her at least once a day. The first time I went, she looked at me and I nodded. That was all. Even after she was able to talk again, she never mentioned Millicent's mirror once, and neither did I.

One day Dad brought in another mirror and hung it on my wall. It was plain, just a round piece of mirrored glass. After he hung it, Dad looked over my shoulder at my face in the mirror. "Don't stop wishing, Lyssie. Not completely."

"But how can I know what to wish?"

Dad smiled and hugged me a little. "You can't. That's what makes life so special."

Even so, I don't wish in this mirror, not like I did the other one. Sometimes when I'm sitting in front of this new flat mirror, practicing my songs for my Saturday morning session with Mr. Birdsong, I remember how Millicent's mirror caught the light. Then I think of the woman who picked the mirror out of the trash, and I wonder if it ever became more than just a mirror to her.

Sometimes I even wish I knew, but it's one of those wishes I don't really want to come true.

ANN GABHART lives on a small farm in Kentucky with her husband and three children. She enjoys bird-watching and walking in the woods and fields with her two dogs. When she's not writing, she's working in her vegetable garden or reading. She's had two historical romances published as well as several novels for teenagers.